A self obsessed bitter twisted middle aged women
A compassionate teenage girl with a cross to bear
And a misogynistic retired police officer

Three people with nothing in common find themselves
trapped together in a hell of their own making
As the story unfolds we see they are not so different
This is a fictional story based on actual events
Where does the fiction end and the truth begin?

*To Cath
Love
John Tait*

CONSCIENCE

Johnny Tait

A Bright Pen Book

Text Copyright © Johnny Tait 2011

Cover design by Jamie Day ©

All rights reserved. No part of this publication may be reproduced, stored in a retrieval system, or transmitted in any form or by any means, electronic, mechanical, photocopy, recording or otherwise, without prior written permission of the copyright owner. Nor can it be circulated in any form of binding or cover other than that in which it is published and without similar condition including this condition being imposed on a subsequent purchaser.

British Library Cataloguing Publication Data.
A catalogue record for this book is available from the British Library

ISBN 978-0-7552-1380-1

Authors OnLine Ltd
19 The Cinques
Gamlingay, Sandy
Bedfordshire SG19 3NU
England

This book is also available in e-book format, details of which are available at www.authorsonline.co.uk

Johnny Tait was born in London's Lambeth Hospital at the Elephant and Castle, and was educated at Archbishop Temple's. At the age of nineteen he joined Butlin's as a Redcoat and has since gone on to make a successful career as a stand-up comedian: a career which has spanned over three decades, giving Johnny the opportunity to appear in some of the best venues in the world.

Conscience is Johnny's first novel, which has also been adapted as a play.

CONTENTS

I AIN'T STAYING LONG 1

NUDITY? IT'S DISGUSTING! 5

MOON LANDINGS AND DROPPING BOMBS 10

THE PREACHER 17

FACELESS AND NAMELESS 30

SNOBS, MORONS AND MOBILE PHONES 32

THE WORST THING THAT CAN HAPPEN TO
A WOMAN 38

RELIGION AND POLITICS 45

WORLD PEACE RALLY 54

SHELLY'S FRIEND 64

CLASS A? 70

FATHER DOESN'T LOVE YOU ANY MORE 72

IT'S A JUBILEE 76

THE ABUSE	79
THOSE HIDEOUS MASKS	92
THE UNOFFICIAL CODE	100
HE BLEW HIS FUCKING HEAD OFF	104
TOMMY	108
HOMO SAPIENS	111
TREVOR THE TRAFFIC	114
JUSTICE	122
JULIE	127
THE WHOLE TRUTH	139
NIGHTMARES	147
A TRIP TO THE SEASIDE	159
MAY THE LORD HAVE MERCY	163

I AIN'T STAYING LONG

There was no odour in the air; there is always an odour, but not now. There was also no sound; listen when you are sitting alone and it's quiet, but there is always sound: it could be birds singing, or the wind rustling through the trees. There is always sound; but here, right now, there was a silence that they had never experienced before.

All around them was darkness, no walls to divide their space from anybody else's space, they could only see each other and the grey stone floor, there was no furniture, just four wooden chairs that had been placed there.

They looked at each other, without acknowledgement, neither one of them knowing where they were or how they got there.

At seventeen years old, Shelly was the youngest; she was 5ft 5in tall, slim with a small frame, she had long natural fair hair that came down past her shoulders, and a fresh unblemished pretty young face that made her attractive in a most natural way, unlike the pin-up girls that look like cardboard cut-outs. Shelly was a natural youthful beauty.

Shelly found the situation she was now in made her feel extremely uneasy; she sat on one of the chairs, she did not feel the need to sit. Finding herself in this eerie situation with two people that she had never met before made her feel so uncomfortable, she did not know what to do, so she just sat down and tried not to catch the eyes of the others.

Have you ever noticed how people will do anything to avoid eye contact with others?

It is particularly noticeable when one is travelling to work on public transport.

Observe the people around you: they will look at a book or a newspaper, or just sit with their eyes half-closed, but they will not make eye contact with anyone around them. Why is that? Are they afraid that if they catch another person's eye it will force them to make polite conversation? Or are we lacking so much in self-confidence that we feel if a stranger speaks to us we will not be able to respond in the correct manner?

Shelly looked at her wristwatch: it had stopped, the second hand was standing still. She tapped it lightly with her index finger, then she slowly shook her wrist. The hands on her wristwatch remained frozen; maybe the tiny battery inside was dead.

It was Fairbanks who broke the silence.

Fairbanks was 5ft 10in tall, medium build, with short dark greying hair; the slight wrinkles in his forehead showed he had seen a bit of life. He was smartly dressed, he was always smartly dressed, wearing a dark grey polyester two-piece suit, a white shirt and a plain navy blue tie; his shoes were black and immaculately polished, you could see your face in them.

Without actually addressing anyone, he stated:

'I don't know how long they expect me to stay here, but I ain't staying long.'

There was a newspaper neatly folded into two on one of the chairs. Fairbanks picked it up, then sat down and started to browse through the pages.

Tilly also sat down. Tilly was 5ft 8in tall, of medium build, with shoulder-length dark hair which she would dye regularly each month in order to stop the very few grey hairs that insisted on popping up from showing. How she hated the fact that the voluptuous figure she had in her younger days was now determined to point south; she had considered having plastic surgery, a boob job, and maybe even liposuction for her rear: she was long past asking the question that all men dread being asked by the woman in his life, "Does my bum look big in this?"

Why do women ask that? What answer is a man supposed to give? If he says, "No, darling, your bum looks lovely in that", the answer he will receive will be, "Why can't you be honest? I hate it when you lie!".

If he says, "I love you, but to be honest your bum looks big in everything", he will incur wrath like he had never dreamed possible.

But Tilly had not asked that question for a long time, as she was fully aware that her bum looked big in everything she wore, but the thing she hated most was that, as a result of a lifetime of yo-yo dieting, she had developed a turkey neck way before her time.

Vanity was Tilly's strongest point or weakest, depending on how we choose to look at it, and she made the maximum effort to look her best at all times.

It was evident from her features that in her youth she would have been an attractive young woman.

NUDITY? IT'S DISGUSTING!

The two women just sat there in silence, not knowing where to look or what to do, not that there was anything for them to do.

Shelly sat there checking the buttons on her white blouse and pulling at the hem of her dark navy blue knee-length skirt, whilst Tilly was continuously checking her dark red painted nails. Fairbanks continued to browse through the newspaper he was holding, then suddenly stated:

'All that money they're wasting sending a man to the moon, it shouldn't be allowed. if God meant man to live on the moon he would of put us there, we would of been born there, but he didn't, and do you know why he didn't?'

He did not ask anyone in particular this question as he did not want a reply from anyone other than himself. He carried on speaking.

'Because he didn't want us to, that's why he didn't, that's why we weren't born on the moon, God don't want us on the moon.'

As he was flicking through the pages, he saw a review for a musical that was playing in a theatre in London's West End. Accompanying the review was a black and white photograph of some of the cast members, and they were all unclothed.

He cried out, 'That's disgusting, dancing around in the nude with no clothes on! Give them all a bloody good haircut and throw them in jail, that's what I say; that's what the money should be spent on, building more jails to throw all these louts in; they should never have stopped national service, if you had national service you wouldn't have none of this long hair and nudity. No, they would have had discipline, that's what they need, discipline. If God meant people to run around nude he would not have given them clothes.'

Even though Fairbanks managed to avoid national service himself, he felt it should never have been abolished, and he blamed everything that he saw wrong in today's youth on the abolishing of national service. The two women looked at each other in astonishment, then at Fairbanks, but very briefly, as neither of them had the desire to catch his eye; they could not understand why he was ranting. Fairbanks turned his attention to Shelly and asked, 'So what do you think? All this dancing around with no clothes on? Disgusting, innit? Shouldn't be allowed. What do you think?'

Shelly was now feeling extremely uncomfortable, she pulled at her skirt. This man was a complete stranger to her and yet here he was asking her what she considered to be an embarrassing question which she had no wish to answer.

Fairbanks persisted. 'It's not natural, is it? People running around naked. What do you reckon? Lock 'em in jail? It's disgusting, innit, ay? What do you say?'

Shelly now felt obliged to answer. 'I would not appear in front of other people with no clothes on myself. I would find that far too embarrassing, but I do not feel that nudity is disgusting. If a show features people naked and the audience are informed that there will be nudity then I don't feel it should be against the law. I read about the show you're talking about at school, during a drama class; it's art.' Fairbanks did not like the answer he was given.

'Art? Art?,' he replied. 'Art is a painting like what Michael Angelo did; not people jumping about with their bits hanging out. What do you know about it anyway? Who asked your opinion?'

Shelly had no desire to reply to Fairbanks. She just sat there, feeling even more uncomfortable, and wondering how she got where she was, and who the other two people were. All she wanted to do was leave, but she did not know how.

MOON LANDINGS AND DROPPING BOMBS

'So what do you think of all this landing on the moon?' Fairbanks asked as he was pointing at the newspaper he was holding, whilst looking in the direction of Shelly.

Shelly did not wish to answer; she was hoping the other woman would respond to his question, but she didn't - she just sat there looking at her nails.

'So what do you think, ay? Do you think they should be landing on the moon? Do yer?'

Once again Shelly felt obliged to answer his question, so she did so in a matter-of-fact way.

'I don't believe that man ever did land on the moon. The evidence shows that at the time the technology was not available. If the heat they would have encountered had not burnt them alive in the spaceship, then they would have died from radiation exposure. A few people said that at the time: in 1967 a man named Thomas Baron inspected the Apollo spaceship and handed in a 500-page report stating that there were a number of flaws in the spacecraft and it was not possible for it to reach the moon. I heard he had also recommended that the programme be aborted, and then eight days later he, his wife and his stepdaughter were killed in an alleged accident when their car got hit by a speeding train close to their home. After Mister Baron's death, the report disappeared.'

Fairbanks was completely baffled by the answer he had just received; normally when he spoke people just said yes or no or just nodded politely. All he wanted to know was whether she thought we should be wasting money sending men to the moon.

He retorted, 'I am not asking for a physics lesson, darling; all I want to know is, do you think we should be sending men to the moon? What are you trying to say? Just answer the question.'

Shelly felt her throat going dry; she wanted a drink, but there was no sign of any beverage. She swallowed. She did not like the man's tone, but answered as politely as she could.

'I studied the alleged moon landings for a project I was doing at school and I don't believe that anybody has ever landed on the moon or ever will.'

Fairbanks stood up and, waving the newspaper in front of Shelly's face, said, 'Of course man landed on the moon! It's there in the paper. What can't talk can't lie, and I watched it on the telly.' We are all familiar with the saying what can't talk can't lie, but even though the tabloid newspapers can't talk, that does not mean they cannot lie.

Whether or not they lied about the moon landing, who knows?

Shelly did not like the way he waved the newspaper in front of her face and did not wish to carry on this conversation any further.

But Fairbanks persisted in a tone as sarcastic as he possibly could manage. 'Come on then, little miss know it all, tell me: if man didn't land on the moon, how come I watched it on telly, ay? Explain that.'

Shelly believed that deep down all people were good and it was wrong to hate anyone, but even though she knew absolutely nothing about this man she could not stop herself from disliking him.

Fairbanks carried on. 'Come on then, if it didn't happen, how come I watched it on the telly?'

Shelly felt compelled to answer. As she spoke, Fairbanks sat back down and crossed his legs.

'I heard it was recorded on a film-set that was built in area 51 of the Nevada desert, then shown around the world as if it were a live recording. The whole thing was an elaborate hoax to con everyone into thinking the Americans had won the race to put a man on the moon.'

Fairbanks looked Shelly straight in the eyes, his facial expression and his body language showing that he was angered by the answers this young girl was giving. 'And why would they do that?' he snapped.

'I don't know why; all I know is that it is unlikely that anyone has ever landed on the moon,' Shelly replied timidly.

'Well, you don't know nothing,' Fairbanks said, once again waving the newspaper at Shelly. 'Of course they landed on the moon; it's there in black and white, and why would the Americans con us into thinking they landed on the moon if they didn't, ay? Come on, tell me why?'

Shelly slowly folded her arms across her chest.

Fairbanks raised his voice.

'Come on, answer the question, why would they say they put a man on the moon if they didn't?'

Shelly reluctantly answered. 'Because the American government want the whole world to believe that they are superior. Russia beat them in the race to put a man into space, so they felt they should go one better. When they discovered that it was not possible to put a man on the moon, they decided to stage it. What the American government are aiming for is world dominance, and they realise that they can't get that just by having the most bombs to create mass destruction, so they go for propaganda, and faking the moon landing was one big propaganda exercise.'

Fairbanks jumped out of his chair and, pointing his finger at Shelly's face, said: 'You really are stupid, and let me tell you about the Americans and their bombs, they're on our side, and if they hadn't have dropped them bombs on the Japanese you'd be talking German. You ain't got a clue about what goes on, have yer?'

Shelly did not understand why this man that she found herself unfortunate enough to be in the company of was reading such an old newspaper, or why he thought that if the American air force had not bombed Japan she would be speaking German. If it were World War Two he was referring to, Germany surrendered in May and the atom bombs were dropped on Hiroshima and Nagasaki four months later. She found his statement totally illogical and did not wish to converse with him any further.

Shelly was a great believer that it was possible for the world to live in peace and was writing a book on how she felt it possible that mankind could live without war, but felt that to try explaining to this self-opinionated man of obvious low intelligence would be a hapless task, so she chose to not say any more.

Whether or not man ever landed on the moon is a debate

that looks as though it will go on forever, or until somebody comes up with conclusive evidence to prove one way or another.

You have probably noticed by now that Fairbanks has an opinion about everything, and he largely gets his information with regards to current affairs from tabloid newspapers.

THE PREACHER

It was the summer of 2012 and the crowds packed into The Royal Albert Hall. There was not an empty seat to be had. So many entertainers have dreamed of playing there, but very few had the fan base to fill the venue. However, tonight five thousand two hundred and fifty people packed into this historic venue to hear the words of the Preacher.

Up until a few weeks ago the Preacher was unheard of, and now everybody wanted to see him, to hear his voice; the sick and the disabled hoped he would cure them.

Nobody knew exactly how many, but there were tens of thousands of people standing outside that could not get a ticket, and so the voice of the Preacher was relayed through a sound system that was set up for the crowds in Kensington Gardens.

'WHO IS HE?
WHERE HAS HE COME FROM?
WHAT IS HIS MESSAGE?
IS HE THE NEW MESSIAH?'

were the front page headlines of the tabloid newspapers that morning, and now they were all here: the camera crews and the journalists.

They came from every national newspaper and every British television channel.

Radio stations were there to broadcast live to their listeners.

The new phenomenon had now hit London and was taking it by storm.

The time was now 8 p.m. Inside the hall the lights dimmed to darkness, the seventy-six piece orchestra started up, and in perfect synchronisation with the music was the most stunning light show ever seen. The crowd inside the great hall were ecstatic; the roar of delight could be heard by the masses outside.

Suddenly the music faded, and the lights dimmed simultaneously.

A white spot of light appeared on the centre of the stage, and standing in the centre of the light was a man that stood six feet tall, was slim of slight to medium build, and had shoulder-length curly dark brown hair; but the most notable feature of his physical appearance was his outstanding big blue eyes that sparkled in the light.

The only clothing he wore was a white loin cloth which was tied around his waist and underneath his crutch in order to cover his genitals. His lightly tanned skin glimmered whilst his arms were outstretched to the side of him, level with his shoulders, the palms of his hands were fully opened, and many of the spectators felt they were seeing Jesus as he was on the cross.

The crowd were in awe of him; everybody's eyes were fixated on him.

There was silence in the great hall; it was so silent one felt that if somebody had dropped a pin at this present moment everybody in the building would have heard it hit the ground.

He addressed his audience. 'Brothers and sisters.'

The crowd leapt to their feet; as they did so they shrieked with delight and clapped their hands together so loudly the sound was deafening, and this carried on for a couple of minutes until the Preacher made a gesture with his hands. The crowd stopped cheering, stopped applauding and slowly sat down to listen to his message.

As he spoke, the crowd held on to his every word.

'Brothers and sisters, I stand before you with no worldly

goods. I have no need for gold or jewellery, I have no need for money or possessions; the only thing I need is your love.'

Again the crowd leapt to their feet, with their sound of approval vibrating around the hall.

He gestured again for them to sit; again they did so, like a well-trained dog obeying his master.

He then carried on speaking, and his voice had a soothing tone.

'Some of you may believe in creation, some may believe in Darwin's theory of evolution. It matters not in which theory you believe. You came into this world with nothing and you will leave this world with nothing. What happens in between is what matters, and that is your decision; yes, you can decide for yourself how to spend your time on earth.

'It matters not what you believe or what you have been taught. What matters is how you treat your fellow beings. Are you going to make the world in which we live a better place? When you leave this mortal soil, will you leave with peace of mind?

'Will you leave feeling that you have done the best you can for the world you are saying farewell to? Will you find your Utopia?'

He paused for a few seconds to give his audience time to contemplate his question; then he carried on speaking and, as he did, he slowly moved around the stage, and he used his hands and his arms to emphasise what he was saying.

'If any person present has never committed a sin, could that person now stand.'

The house lights went up, he paused and looked around, but everybody remained seated. After a few seconds he spoke again.

'Of course, nobody is standing. We have all sinned, but how do we repent?

'How do we cleanse ourselves of our sins?

'Does praying for forgiveness put right the wrong we have done? I do not think so. "Thou shall not kill." If I asked anybody to name me the ten commandments, that is one of the ten that I am sure everybody would remember. If I ask any of you, "Have you ever killed?", you would reply, "No, I would never do that".

'But have you? Have you ever been responsible for another person's death?

'I heard of a young mother aged just twenty-eight that recently passed away from cancer, leaving behind two grieving children, deprived of their mother's love. Are you to blame?

'Could you have done anything to prevent her death?

'Stand up if you are sure that you are in no way to blame.'

Everybody remained seated, except for one man that had been sitting five rows back from the stage. He stood up, bold and upright.

The Preacher caught sight of him, and asked for somebody to give the man a microphone to enable him to speak so that all persons present could hear.

A floor walker immediately approached him and handed him a radio mic.

The man took the microphone but did not speak. The Preacher asked him, 'Do you feel that you are in no way responsible for that young woman's death? Do you feel that there is nothing you could have done to prevent the early passing of her young life?'

The man lifted the microphone to his mouth and stated, 'I do not know the woman you are talking about. I have never met her, and until now had never ever heard anything about her, so how can I be responsible?'

The Preacher looked at the man and said, 'My brother, firstly I commend you for being brave enough to protest your innocence before so many people.

'There are probably a thousand people amongst this congregation that feel they are in no way to blame, but you, my brother, have found the courage to say so. May I ask you a question?'

The man standing nodded his head.

'Are you aware that the National Health Service is underfunded?'

He did not speak, he just nodded.

'Are you in gainful employment?'

Again the response was just a nod.

'Am I right to presume that you pay income tax?'

Once again the reply he received was just a nod.

'So let me ask you, let me ask all of you, do you not feel that you should be allowed to say how your money is spent? Collectively the people inside this hall pay millions of pounds every year in taxes, yet people are dying needlessly because our National Health Service is underfunded. And you just sit back and allow it to happen.

'The Silverback Gorilla, the Snow Leopard and many other living species are in danger of extinction, but what do you do about it?

'You sit back and allow it to happen. Do not feel guilt, for you are not the guilty.

'But ask yourselves this question: what can I do about it? How can I improve our National Health Service to prevent the unnecessary death of a young person?

'How can I save the beautiful creatures that have been put on this planet from extinction? Brothers and sisters, whether you believe our planet and the life forms that inhabit it were put here by God or Mother Nature, I am sure you will agree that we must take responsibility for the survival of every living species.'

He paused and the audience applauded. The Preacher looked at the man standing; his expression invited him to speak.

A spotlight was pointing at the man standing, and everybody's eyes were fixated on him. He nervously lifted the microphone to his mouth and stated, 'But how can I be responsible? There is nothing I can do. I go to work, I pay my bills and at the end of the month I have very little if anything at all left in my bank account.

'How can I improve the National Health Service, or save the Silverback Gorilla?'

There was silence around the Albert Hall. The eyes of everyone present now turned back towards the Preacher. They all had their ears pricked waiting for his reply. He smiled and answered.

'Brothers and sisters, most of you have little left in your bank accounts at the end of each month, but you do not need to suffer any financial hardship in order to make your world a better place.'

The Preacher paused for a few seconds, then he began to explain.

'You calculate the sum you are due to pay the Inland Revenue, then you send a big fat cheque for that amount to whichever cause that you feel you would prefer to financially support. You then send a copy of your accounts, along with a photocopy of that cheque, to the taxman, informing him of the way in which you have paid your income tax.

'How many people here would like to donate all of the money they give to the Inland Revenue to the Great Ormond Street Hospital for Children?'

In reply to his question, a large section of the audience cheered and enthusiastically clapped their hands together.

'How many of you would like to save our endangered species from extinction?'

Again his question was met with emphatic applause.

'Brothers and sisters, you can make your world a better place, you can build Heaven here on Earth; it is within your power to create Utopia.'

The assembly stood and cheered enthusiastically. After a couple of minutes, the Preacher gestured for the people to sit; they sat and waited for him to speak again. A presenter for a national radio station that was transmitting live to its listeners described the Preacher as 'A man who has a command over an audience that no person in the history of humankind has ever had'.

The Preacher continued to speak in his soft, soothing tone. 'Of course, Utopia cannot be built with finances alone. In order to create the perfect world we must begin with ourselves.

Are any of us present today in this great hall responsible for the violence in our society? I see many of you are shaking your head in order to indicate no. I would like you to stand if you have ever struck another person in anger.'

The majority of the people in the hall rose to their feet.

'I would like you people to remain standing for a moment. Stand up if you have ever raised your voice in anger to another person.'

The remainder of the people were now on their feet.

'Look around you and you will see you are not the only person standing. Everybody is standing, because we are all responsible for the violence in our society and we must all take the responsibility to end it upon ourselves, by denouncing any form of violence and vowing to never react violently towards any other person ever again.

'As the world's most famous pacifist said, "If someone slaps you on the right cheek, turn the other cheek to him as well".'

The crowd were screaming and applauding their approval.

After a minute or so the Preacher indicated for the people to sit. He then smiled and said, 'Stand up if you consider yourself to be beautiful.'

He paused and slowly looked around the hall; everybody else did likewise, and as they did so they began to laugh.

'Nobody is standing. Is that because nobody considers themselves to be beautiful? Or is it because nobody is brave enough to say look at me, I'm beautiful?'

The audience laughed. The Preacher then pointed to a young woman in her mid-twenties who was sitting in the second row and said, 'I would like to ask you a question; would you stand up please?'

As he did so, a floor-walker rushed over to her and held a microphone to her mouth. The Preacher continued.

'Would you kindly tell us all why you do not consider yourself to be beautiful.'

As she answered she giggled. 'Because I've got a big bum.'

Everybody else laughed along with her. The Preacher smiled and asked, 'Does anybody else here consider themselves to have a big bum?'

Everybody laughed as a large percentage of the women stood.

The Preacher asked them to sit; then, pointing to a man in the seventh row, he asked, 'And why do you not consider yourself to be beautiful?'

'Because I've got a big nose,' the man replied.

In a cheerful yet self-mocking way, some of the people laughed and clapped their hands as to show appreciation of his ability to make fun of himself.

Then, pointing to a teenage girl in the fourth row, the

Preacher asked, 'How is it possible for someone as young as your good self to not be beautiful?'

The girl mumbled into the microphone the floor-walker was holding as she replied, 'I've got spots.'

Nobody laughed at the young girl's statement, for suddenly everybody felt a sense of embarrassment.

'I would like to ask you all a question.'

As he said that he held his arms outstretched in front of him and moved them outwards until they were level with his shoulders.

'Is the largest land mammal on earth, the African Elephant, beautiful?' The reply from the auditorium was 'Yes'.

'I did not hear you; is the Elephant beautiful?'

The crowd now roared 'Yes'.

'Is what has been described an exotic bird, the Parrot beautiful?'

'Yes!'

'Is the Leopard beautiful?'

'Yes!'

'The Elephant has a big bum, the Parrot's got a big nose, the Leopard's got spots, and they are all beautiful. All of God's creations are beautiful. All of Mother Nature's creatures are beautiful, and you, brothers and sisters, are beautiful. Stand up if you are beautiful.'

Everybody now stood and cheered enthusiastically.

'Brothers and sisters, we can support our health service, we can save all the world's creatures from extinction, we can live in a world without violence, we can live in Utopia.

As the world's second most famous pacifist said, "I have a dream".

'And together we can make our dream come true.'

The masses outside the hall as well as inside were screaming ecstatically; they could be heard for miles across London.

FACELESS AND NAMELESS

It was an emergency meeting. The five men present were summoned just a few hours earlier. Nobody liked being woken at four in the morning, they sat there solemn faced, around the mahogany oval-shaped table, the thick deep red velvet curtains were pulled shut, blocking out the early morning light, the small crystal chandelier hanging over the centre of the table lit up the dull conference room, the walls were painted chocolate brown, on one side was a three foot by two foot oil painting of a hunting scene, the rest of the walls were bare.

'This is the biggest threat to our institution ever, and what are we going to do about it?

'That lunatic will not just bring down the government, he will destroy everything we stand for.'

'Did you hear the results of the survey? Forty percent of

the population are saying they will no longer pay income tax, but will donate the sum due to charity.'

'They are likening him to Jesus Christ.'

'We must terminate him before he does any more damage.'

'If he were to be killed in a freak accident, or die under suspicious circumstances, they would make him a martyr; the last thing we need is a bloody martyr.'

'The best way to deal with this is to discredit him. Leave it to me. Within the next forty-eight hours, the problem will have gone away.'

No names have been mentioned.

No person physically described.

That is because these men are faceless, nameless; yet they make decisions that not only affect the lives of individuals, but affect the lives of whole nations.

They stood, nodded their heads in acknowledgment of each other and quietly left the room.

SNOBS, MORONS AND MOBILE PHONES

Fairbanks turned his attention to Tilly. 'So, what do you reckon. ay? Should we be wasting money sending men to the moon? Or should we be building more prisons to get the scum off the streets?'

Tilly was choosy about whom she spoke with; she preferred to only associate with people of wealth and had absolutely no desire to converse with a man wearing cheap mass-produced high street clothing.

'What's a matter, can't you speak or has the cat got your tongue?' Fairbanks asked.

Tilly now answered, looking down her nose at Fairbanks as if he were a bad smell and sounding as if she had half a dozen plums in her mouth.

'I can speak and the cat has not got my tongue. I just

choose not to answer your ridiculous question.'

'Oh golly gosh,' replied Fairbanks; then, doing his best to mimic her, he repeated: 'I can speak and the cat has not got my tongue. I just choose not to answer your ridiculous question.'

Then, dropping the fake posh voice and returning to his native south London accent, he looked her straight in the eye and said, 'Fucking snob.'

Then he opened the newspaper and carried on flicking through it.

It was now silent; the only sound was that of the turning pages of the newspaper.

Shelly was carrying a small black imitation leather handbag. She put her hand inside and took out her mobile phone. The screen was blank; she tried to switch it on, but it did not respond.

This led her to thinking about the time a mobile phone company had billed her for £180 more than she owed them. She had tried on numerous occasions to explain that there had obviously been a mistake, but to no avail.

When a person has been overcharged by a mobile phone company, the procedure is: you phone them, your call will get you through to an animated machine, the voice will give you options as to which numbered button you should press on your handset to put you through to the service you require, you then press the number on the keypad of your handset, then the animated voice speaks to you again and gives you more options; this procedure repeats itself three or four times, before the animated voice instructs you to please hold while we put you through to one of our customer service team; you are then subjected to at least five minutes of listening to nauseating music till eventually a complete moron who does not give a shit that you have been overcharged answers your call with the words, 'You are through to customer services; Chris speaking, how can I help you?'

You now explain to Chris that there has obviously been a mistake with your bill as you never go over your inclusive minutes and you have not travelled abroad or made any calls abroad, or dialled any premium rate numbers.

The moron you have called does not know how to answer your enquiry, so he asks you to hold while he connects you to somebody on the customer service team that can help you.

You are now subjected to more nauseating music till a voice on the end of the line says, 'Customer services; you are through to Vicky, how may I help you?'

Vicky is similar to Chris in the fact that she is also a complete moron and she also does not give a shit about the fact that you have been overcharged by £180. But she has worked for the company longer than Chris and has been trained to sound as if she is sympathetic about your problem.

You now have to explain all over again that there has been an obvious mistake with your bill as Vicky does not know what you said to Chris. When you have finished explaining, Vicky will say, 'Can you hold while I connect you to somebody that can help with your enquiry?'

This farce carries on till you get angry or frustrated and hang up the phone, or in some cases till the caller gets so annoyed that he or she loses patience and swears at the customer service moron, who then terminates the call, as he or she has been instructed that they have a right to do if the caller uses foul or abusive language.

Shelly never used foul or abusive language; she just attempted on four separate occasions to explain that there had been a mistake with her bill.

Then one day a letter arrived threatening her with legal action if she did not pay up.

Again Shelly called the mobile phone company and tried again to explain that there had been a mistake. Her Grandmother overheard the conversation she was having, and could see she was upset, and knew that even if Shelly did owe this money she would have had no means to pay it. Shelly's Gran took the bill from her and said, 'Don't worry, I'll pay it. It use to be that thieves would pull stockings over their heads and carry shotguns to rob banks; now they just set up mobile phone companies and bill people for amounts of money they don't owe, and the law allows them to do it. What is the world coming to?'

Fairbanks sat there looking at Shelly as she sat there staring at the blank screen on her mobile phone. 'What's that thing you're holding there?' he asked, pointing his finger.

'My mobile phone,' answered Shelly.

'What's a mobile phone?' Fairbanks asked.

Tilly just shook her head, and muttered under her breath, 'Ignoramus'.

THE WORST THING THAT CAN HAPPEN TO A WOMAN

For a few moments there was silence, nobody speaking. Fairbanks was quietly browsing through the newspaper and the two women were feeling grateful for that. The silence was broken by Tilly trying to make small talk to ease the boredom, as she turned towards Shelly and said, 'I hope they don't keep us here for too long.'

'Me too,' was Shelly's reply.

'So what do you do?' Tilly asked.

'I'm still at school taking my A levels. I'm hoping to go to university.'

Tilly replied, 'That is the one thing I regret, not going to university. I have heard its excellent fun. They say it's the best social life you'll ever have, meeting lots of like-minded people, having a good time going into bars and drinking lots of alcohol.'

'I don't really drink much,' replied Shelly, 'and I very rarely go into a pub. Besides, I'm only seventeen and I always get asked for my identification.'

'I don't go into bars that often myself,' said Tilly. 'The thing is, they are full of poor people. I have no time for poor people; they don't need to be poor, nobody needs to be poor. If they just got off their big fat council-house behinds, and got their big fat blotchy council-house legs to take them out and do something about it, then they would not be poor, and the achievers in this world would not have to listen to them complaining about the cost of this and the price of that.

'And they call themselves working class. I have no desire to socialise with the working class.'

Shelly chose not to reply to this statement, as she totally disagreed with Tilly's social view.

In order for society to function as we know it, it needs people that are prepared to do the low-paid manual labour tasks. What would happen if we did not have anybody that was prepared to sweep the roads, or empty our rubbish bins or drive our buses?

Those of us with common sense are grateful that we have people that are prepared to do the low-paid work that we would not like to do ourselves, but Tilly liked to think of them as beneath her. She saw most people as beneath her; it was one of the things that made her feel good about herself, and just looked down on them.

Everybody has a role to play in our society and every person is just as important as the next.

As Shelly had not commented on Tilly's last statement, she decided to carry on. 'You know, I was in a bar one night and this man came up to me, still wearing his working overalls, beer belly, unshaven, repulsive sight he was, and he said to me, "Is that a ladder in your tights or a stairway to heaven?". How corny is that?

'Did he really expect me to be impressed? So I went straight back at him. I said it's a stairway to heaven, but I've already got one arsehole in my knickers, thank you very much, so crawl back into the gutter where you belong.

'He didn't have an answer for that, so he just slithered away, pathetic little creature. When I go out with the girls I want to be able to sit at the bar and drink without being disturbed by some nasty little lowlife.'

Fairbanks put down the newspaper he was reading, and, shaking his head in disgust, he proclaimed, 'It never use to be like that. A lady was a lady. She knew how to behave, everybody knew where they stood, there was none of this women standing at the bar and getting pissed; they knew their place.'

When Fairbanks was younger, it was unheard of for a

woman to go to the pub unless she was accompanied by her husband, and even then she would not have dreamed of standing at the bar: she would sit quietly at a table and only speak when spoken to; and you would never have seen a woman in a pub during the Sunday lunchtime session, husband or no husband; it was not the law, it was just the way things were, and Fairbanks believed that was how it should always be.

'A man could go to the pub and enjoy a pint with no jukebox, no pool table or any of that noise and when he got home his dinner was on the table. That was the whole point of having a wife. Nowadays the pubs are full of women; who's at home cooking the dinner?'

Tilly was not going to let a sexist comment like that go unchastised. Throwing her arms out with the palms of her hands stretched, she said, 'That was the whole point of having a wife, so that your dinner was on the table when you got home from the pub? So tell me, why would a woman want a husband?'

Fairbanks stood up and, raising his arms in the air, he proclaimed, 'It's what being a woman is all about. I pity any woman who's not married by the time she reaches 25.'

He then pulled a chair closer to where Shelly was sitting, and then, as he sat down, he put his right hand on her left knee and carried on. 'You see, if a girl keeps herself decent,' then nodding his head as if he wanted Shelly to nod in agreement, 'You know what I mean by decent?' Fairbanks felt that every woman should remain a virgin till the day she wed, because in his view the best thing a young woman has to offer a man is her chastity. Of course, it was all right for a young man to sow his wild oats - after all, that was what being a young man is all about, it's nature - but a young lady should be untouched until her wedding day. 'You know what I mean by decent?' he repeated, nodding his head again.

Shelly did not know how to respond, so she just nodded her head sheepishly.

He carried on. 'And if she don't go getting too fat, she'll be lucky enough to get married; you see, when a young lady finds herself a man to cook for, and clean for, and to have his babies, she's got it ... made, she's got it made.'

Shelly did not like this man touching her and found the way he put his face so close to her's quite intimidating; despite that, she felt that she should reply to his statement.

'Daddy did most of the cooking in our house; he was an excellent cook and he enjoyed doing it.'

Fairbanks never once saw his father cook and he never cooked himself.

When his wife was in hospital following the birth of his son, he ate his breakfast in the local cafe and brought his dinner home from the fish and chip shop in the high street.

As soon as his wife returned from hospital, she was back in the kitchen.

The thought of a man cooking when he had a wife at home that was perfectly capable of doing so angered him.

He pressed his face closer to Shelly's and in a voice much louder than necessary stated, 'Well, he shouldn't! Your mum should do all the cooking and while she's doing it she should be teaching you.'

Shelly pulled her face away from his as far as she possibly could, although she remained seated, and replied timidly, 'My Mum can't do that because she's ...'

Fairbanks did not allow her to finish; he just shouted back at her. 'Well, your mother should do that; you need to learn so you can cook for your husband.'

Tilly had heard enough; she was not prepared to sit back and listen to his ranting any longer.

'What a load of nonsense,' she bellowed.

Fairbanks now turned his anger towards Tilly. 'Nonsense? Nonsense? It ain't nonsense! The worst thing that can happen to a woman is for no one to marry her, 'cause having a husband is what being a woman is all about. You see, man is the superior being and it's a woman's place to serve him.'

Shelly intercepted timidly. 'I don't think that's right. Daddy always said everybody is equal.'

RELIGION AND POLITICS

Even though he only ever attended church for weddings and funerals, Fairbanks would often refer to God, and he would claim to be a Christian, despite the fact that he was quite ignorant of what the Christian faith is all about. He felt he knew everything there was to know. Thinking 'I know everything there is to know' is common amongst ignorant people; their ignorance makes them unaware that they are ignorant. Fairbanks felt he understood Christianity fully and that it was right that he should regularly quote the bible.

He believed the reason for all the inns being full when Jesus was born was because it was Christmas.

And the reason Jesus was crucified on Good Friday was because the Romans thought that more people would be there to see it as it was the Easter holidays.

And that the reason Palm Sunday was named Palm Sunday was because it was the only day of the year that men of the cloth were permitted to masturbate.

He also felt that by claiming to be a Christian he would automatically gain entry into Heaven.

Fairbanks began to preach. 'You see, we worship God and we serve God because God is our creator.'

Tilly asked sarcastically, 'And what has any of that got to do with who does the cooking?'

Fairbanks jumped up from his seat and, pointing to his chest, declared, 'God is a man.'

Tilly responded by jumping up and saying, 'I don't believe that God is either a man or a woman and if …'

Fairbanks did not allow her to finish. He ranted: 'God made man in the image of himself; if God were a woman, it would say God made man in the image of herself.'

Tilly shook her head as she sat back in her seat. Shelly looked on bewildered. Fairbanks carried on with his sermon.

'So God made man to serve him, and he called that man Adam because Adam means the first one. Now, the man - the hunter-gatherer - wanted someone to serve him, and cook for him and clean for him, so he took out one of his ribs and from that rib he created woman, and that is how you get the name woman, because you came from the womb of a man, womb-man-woman.

'And Adam gave her the name Eve because he knew it would be easy for her to spell.

'And for millions of years a man and his wife lived happily together till along came some stupid tart wanting the vote and that was where it all went wrong.'

Tilly laughed in a mocking way. She had grown to realise that there was one thing men did not like and that was being mocked, and Fairbanks certainly did not like it, especially from a woman.

He clenched his fist in anger and retorted, 'You can laugh, you can laugh, but there weren't no divorce in them days, and why? In three words I'll tell you why: Love, Honour and Obey.'

Tilly held up four fingers in front of his face and said in a mocking tone 'That's four words.'

'Do what?'

Tilly then put up one finger, 'Love', then a second finger, 'Honour', a third, 'and', a fourth, 'Obey; that's four words.'

Fairbanks was not used to being spoken to in this way, and certainly not by a woman. There was one occasion when his wife had spoken to him in this tone, so he slapped her, not hard enough to do her any harm, but enough to show her who's boss; he slapped his wife whenever he felt that she had stepped out of line, and felt that was what made his marriage work. And now he was taking abuse from a woman he had only just met, he wanted to slap her, but he didn't: he just yelled.

'Oh yeh, you can take the piss, but it was when women stopped obeying that our country went to the dogs; now we've got people on the dole, kids carrying guns and knives, homeless people begging on the streets, graffiti all over the walls and ...'

Tilly did not allow him to finish. She interrupted: 'What has that got to do with a woman not obeying her sexist, ignoramus husband?'

Fairbanks yelled back, 'Everything! Now we got girls wearing jeans and having tattoos, and men with long hair ... right bunch of poofs they all look.'

Against her better judgement, Shelly joined in the debate; even though she did not like this kind of heated discussion, she felt it her duty as a human being to speak up if any person or group of people were being unfairly discriminated against. She spoke very quietly.

'I don't think you can judge a man's sexuality by the length of his hair, and I don't understand why you're being so homophobic; some of my best friends are gay.'

Shelly may well have been speaking Russian or Chinese or any other language that Fairbanks did not understand, because he certainly did not understand the language she was speaking now. As far as he was concerned, if a man did not dress and behave in a way he considered a man should, then he was a poof, it was as simple as that.

Shelly speaking to him in this way angered him; he spoke to her through gritted teeth.

'Homophobic, homophobic, what kind of a word is that? And why do you call them gay? Gay means happy, not "I want to stick it up another man's arse".'

Shelly was completely taken aback by this. She was brought up to respect her elders, which she did, but now this man who was more than old enough to be her father, was waving his arms about and speaking to her in a way in which she found completely disrespectful.

It was Tilly that intervened. Looking Fairbanks straight in the eye, she said: 'Why don't you shut up, you stupid old fool; and what the hell am I doing here listening to your crap?'

'Crap? It ain't crap, and if you listen - if everybody listens - we will put the world right, because we are the ones that bring law and order to this world; without us the human race would wipe itself out or die of starvation.'

'Us? Us? Who are us?' asked Tilly, not really wanting a reply, but she got one all the same.

'Who are us? Who are us? Who do you think, you stupid posh tart; us, the British men, we are the providers of the world, we keep things on the straight and narrow and without us to lead, the rest of the world would be dead.'

Shelly had never heard a posh lady swear before, but she was going to now as Tilly exclaimed, 'That is the biggest load of bollocks I have ever heard.'

Fairbanks retaliated. 'Bollocks! It's not bollocks ... listen ... Now listen ... when Britain was Great Britain we didn't have any women in Parliament, we had men ruling not just our own country but the rest of the world: Winston Churchill, Richard the Lionheart, Henry the Eighth.

'You see, the Queen, God bless her heart, is a lovely woman, but that's what she is - a woman - and women cannot rule. Oh no, what we need is a man on the throne. Then we will be great again. When we were a kingdom we were ruled by a king.'

Tilly just pulled a face and said, 'When we were an empire, we were ruled by an emperor, now we are a country.'

It went quiet for a while. Fairbanks was trying to figure out what she was saying.

Then Shelly quietly offered some information.

'Henry the Eighth introduced divorce.'

'What?'

'You mentioned Henry the Eighth. The Catholic church would not sanction divorce, so he founded The Church of England, and then he made himself head of it, and introduced divorce.'

Fairbanks did not like her statement at all; one of the

things he was proud of and, in his view, knew everything about was the Church of England. He spoke through gritted teeth.

'What a load of rubbish. I'll tell you who invented divorce, it was that bloody lesbian Emily Parkhurst, she's the one that invented divorce; didn't like the idea of a man and his wife living happily together, no, so she invents divorce, totally destroyed family life, and do you know what they did? They went and named a bloody prison after her, that's what they did.'

Tilly could not miss the opportunity to anger him even further. She laughed and rocked back and forth in a mocking way. 'It's Pankhurst, you stupid old fool, not Parkhurst.'

'It's Parkhurst,' Fairbanks bellowed. 'Parkhurst! I should know, I sent enough low-life scumbags there.'

Shelly foolishly attempted to educate him. 'Emmeline Pankhurst; she was one of the founders of the suffragettes.'

'Pankhurst, Parkhurst, that's not the point; the point is that bloody lesbian started divorce.'

Emmeline Goulden was born in 1858 and twenty years later married Richard Pankhurst, a barrister twenty years her senior, who was known for supporting women's rights movements.

The now Emmeline Pankhurst campaigned tirelessly for equal votes for women and, on numerous occasions, she and members of the group found themselves arrested and imprisoned. In 1913 a fellow campaigner (thirty-year-old Emily Davison) lost her life when, during the Epsom Derby, she threw herself under the King's horse. Just before she did so she shouted 'Votes for women'. Many women devoted their lives and some gave their lives for their cause.

In 1918 women over the age of thirty were granted the right to vote. Shortly after, the age for women to vote was lowered to twenty-one, as it was at that time for men.

In those days people thought that voting meant that the people of Britain could have their say in the running of their country.

It was many years later that people began to realise that going to the polling station with your ballot paper in your hand did not give you a say in the running of your country; it merely helped to massage the inflated ego of the candidate you voted for.

And, of course, it leads us all into thinking we live in a democracy.

In time, people will realise that, if Parliament decides to pass a bill that they know the majority of people do not want, it will not make any difference - they will pass it all the same.

And if the government wish to risk the lives of the young men and women serving in our armed forces by starting an unnecessary war, they will do so with or without our blessing.

'Emmeline Pankhurst was married with five children; she never got divorced,' said Shelly. 'Argh, ha ha, see,' said Tilly, waving her finger in front of Fairbanks, 'Emily bloody Parkhurst, ha ha ha.'

Fairbanks would not be corrected by anyone; he retorted, 'It was Parkhurst and she invented divorce. That's the trouble these days, bloody schools, they don't teach you kids nuffing.'

Using the worst possible accent Tilly could speak in, she repeated, 'don't teach you kids nuffing. It's a pity your school didn't teach you nuffing; I've never heard such appalling grammar.'

'If there's one thing I can't stand it's a bloody posh tart,' replied Fairbanks.

Feeling that she should have the last word, Tilly stated, 'And if there's one thing I can't stand, it's an ignoramus old bigot like you.'

WORLD PEACE RALLY

Shelly's favourite subject was history: as well as it being her first choice subject at school, she would study it in her spare time; she also took a keen interest in current affairs and always made a point of watching the news programmes on television.

Every Thursday she would attend a debating group where they would discuss world events, both past and current. There were usually between sixteen and twenty people at these meetings, the youngest being Shelly and the oldest was Luke, who was aged twenty-six.

Shelly had become particular friendly with Martin, a young man that was four years her senior and who shared similar interests: they would spend days together visiting art galleries; they also shared an interest in live theatre.

If ever there was a campaigner for peace it was Martin;

whenever there was a conflict anywhere in the world, he would question, 'Is this really *necessary?*'

Then, before anybody answered, he would add, 'Of course, violence is never the answer.'

His all-time hero was the civil rights activist Martin Luther King, whom his mother said he was named after. He admired him for the fact that he was not afraid to speak up for what he believed and at the same time denounced violence.

Martin had a warm sense of humour and would ask questions like, 'What would Martin Luther King have said in his famous speech if he had been an insomniac?'

And he would make statements like, 'Fighting for peace is like fucking for virginity'.

When Martin was a child, his father died from injuries he received during the Falklands conflict.

During the taking of Goose Green, his father (Private Wight) was injured when a shell exploded in front of him; he was treated for severe head injuries and heavy blood loss.

After spending four weeks in hospital, Private Wight was medically discharged from the army and was presented with the South Atlantic medal.

Four months later, Private Wight was fortunate to land a well-paid job in London's Fleet Street. He married his sweetheart Catherine, they had five children, and he now had everything he wished for - becoming a family man was the only ambition he ever had.

It was twenty-four years later, when Martin was twelve years old, that his father started to suffer as a result of the small pieces of shrapnel that were left inside his head.

It began with epileptic fits, then he became paralysed down his left side, and this was followed by losing his eyesight and going completely blind.

In the last two weeks of his life Martin's father was in a hospice, where he was cared for by nuns; he was in so much pain that he was given large doses of morphine, so much that he did not know where he was. At the age of forty-nine, Martin's father passed away.

Seeing his father suffer in this way left a massive scar on Martin; he suffered from severe bouts of depression, but never did he feel any kind of sympathy for himself.

He would regularly preach that no person should ever suffer the way his father had, and no children should experience the grief he saw in his brothers and sisters.

At one of the debating meetings somebody had stated that both the American and the British governments want people to believe that certain countries are a threat to world peace in order to give them an excuse to invade a country that refuses to trade with them on their terms.

The members of the debating group of which Shelly

belonged all wanted world peace and they all believed that we are all being brainwashed by our governments.

In their debating group everything was discussed in a civilised manner.

Among the comments Shelly had heard were:

'They didn't do any good in Vietnam; in fact, they did a lot of bad.'

'So what good are they going to do over there?'

'If they are terrorists, then why have we been supplying them with arms?'

'That has to be the greatest miscarriage of justice ever.'

'We won't ever know why he was hung, because they won't ever tell us the truth.'

'If anybody else did that, he or she would be put in prison, but he has got off scot free, and do you know why? Because he's a policeman, that's why.'

'Our governments are trying to brainwash us into thinking all Muslims are terrorists. I have met a lot of Muslims and do you know what, they are all nice people.'

Four days after the gathering in the Royal Albert Hall, the debating group got together.

They were all excited about the arrival of the Preacher, and felt that he had the answers

to everything that was wrong in the world.

Somebody raised the point that he had organised a world

peace march through London at the weekend, and, as the one thing they all had in common was that they wanted world peace, they should all go along.

Everybody agreed that it would be a good way to meet like-minded people, and, if there was anything worth standing up and being counted for, it was peace.

So Shelly and her friends from the debating group met at the local British Rail station early on the Sunday morning and took the train into London.

During the march everybody was in high spirits; it was a warm and sunny day, with most of the people wearing t-shirts with various slogans on them.

We can save the Whale
Stand up for peace
Everybody's Beautiful
He is here on Earth

were among the slogans on the t-shirts the people were wearing.

As they walked, they were chanting a line from a well-known John Lennon song, 'All we are saying is give peace a chance'.

They passed various television camera crews and as they did they chanted even louder and almost everybody raised one arm in the air to give a peace sign.

They had been walking and chanting for over a hour now and Shelly was enjoying the day and looking forward to seeing the Preacher, and to hearing him speak, and was excited about the party and the live music in Hyde Park that was to follow the rally.

Suddenly, a group of twenty to twenty-five men wearing black balaclavas that completely covered their faces joined the march; they were shouting in an aggressive tone, 'Kill kill kill the bill'. They were carrying house bricks and long pieces of wood, and started to smash the windows of the buildings around them. The happiness that Shelly felt had now turned into sheer horror. S,he felt one of her friends grab her arm and shout at the top of his voice 'Let's get away from here'. The group she was with started to run, to get away from these disruptive thugs that were hell bent on turning a peaceful orderly rally into a violent disruptive one.

As they were trying to get away from the thugs that they in no way wanted to be associated with, the police, wearing full riot kit and carrying shields and batons, charged at them.

Shelly, along with many others, was knocked to the floor. A feeling of sheer panic came over her; she did not know how to react, she just put her hands on her head and pulled her knees up to her chest and just lay there in the foetal position.

As Shelly lay there, she could hear screaming and people

shouting, but was unable to determine what anybody was trying to say.

The short time she was on the ground seemed like forever; then a friend from her debating group knelt beside her and, putting his hand on her shoulder, said, 'It's all right, Shelly, stand up.'

Shelly opened her eyes and saw it was Joseph, one of the members of her debating group. He was nineteen years old, a bit taller than Shelly, and extremely slim, with black thin shoulder-length hair. Joseph always spoke quietly with a soft gentle voice.

Shelly got to her feet, but as she did so she saw the police putting one of her friends into the back of a police van: why they had arrested Martin nobody knew, he wouldn't harm a fly, and had to be the most inoffensive person anybody could possibly meet.

Martin's ambition was to become a drama teacher and he had been successful in a recent application and was due to start the job he had dreamed of when term time resumed.

The thugs wearing balaclavas had now disappeared down a side street and Shelly, along with approximately one thousand other world peace marchers, found themselves surrounded by police. Some of the people tried to protest to the police that the way they were being detained in which the police called kettling was unlawful; they were either punched or had the policemen's riot shields pushed in their faces.

After a couple of hours, Shelly witnessed a young woman approach one of the kettling police and say, 'Will you let me go now? I need to use the lavatory.' The policeman hit her on the side of her knees with his truncheon, sending her sprawling to the ground.

Five and a half hours passed before the police would allow the world peace marchers to leave; during that time they were offered no food or drink, and Shelly, along with many others, had completely lost control of her bladder.

The following day the headlines in the national newspapers read

'PEACE MARCH DESCENDS INTO A RIOT. POLICE MAKE DOZENS OF ARRESTS'

Martin appeared in court charged with criminal damage and assaulting a police officer, and even though everybody knew he was innocent he was found guilty and received a six-months custodial sentence.

He was not allowed to proceed with his career as a drama teacher.

None of the thugs wearing balaclavas were ever caught or arrested.

No police officer faced any charges or disciplinary action whatsoever.

Never again did Shelly or any of her friends take part in any other rally.

SHELLY'S FRIEND

'I wish you weren't so nasty to each other. I don't like it when people are nasty to each other,' Shelly said in a timid manner.

'I bet you've never done anything nasty in your life,' replied Tilly.

Shelly's heart seemed to sink as she stated, 'I did once and I regret it now. There was a girl at my school. She was different from all the other girls; I don't mean she looked different, she just seemed like the odd one out. She was quiet, like she never said anything unless you asked her a question, then she just sort of answered, but didn't say much, just yes or no mostly; she always seemed embarrassed. She played the violin, and was really good at it; she would regularly visit old people's homes and play for the residents, and was a member of a youth orchestra: they even played a big charity concert at the Royal Albert Hall.

'I never understood why, but some of the girls would pick on her and call her names; the ugly duckling was their favourite, but she wasn't ugly in any way: she had the most adorable sparkling eyes, a lovely complexion with the most amazing skin tone, and soft silky chestnut hair; personally I thought she was beautiful.

'But just because she was quiet, the girls would call her names and knock her books out of her hand.'

Fairbanks interrupted. 'She should have stood up to them and made them stop.'

'She wasn't like that; she would not have wanted confrontation,' replied Shelly.

'So why didn't *you* make them stop?' As he asked, Fairbanks was pointing his finger at Shelly. Shelly was now feeling uneasy and as she spoke she pulled at the hem of her skirt in a way as if she was just looking for something else to do other than answer the accusing question that had been put to her. 'I wanted to, but I was afraid if I did they would bully me as well.'

Fairbanks was now pointing his finger a couple of inches from Shelly's chest as he spoke. 'Surely, if she was your friend you would have wanted to help her.'

'I really did like her,' said Shelly defensively. 'There were a number of times when we would catch each other's eye and I would kind of smile at her and she would smile back; it gave me butterflies in my tummy. I could see she wanted to be my friend, but we never really spoke to each other; there were many times when I wanted to speak with her, but I never had the courage to go up to her and do so. Then one day, during lunch break, I was in the school dining room when she came and sat next to me and we starting talking. It was so nice to have a proper conversation with her. She spoke very quietly, almost in a whisper, and she told me her Mum worked at the local theatre and that the "Rocky Horror" show was on there the following week and that she had two complimentary tickets for the opening night and asked me if I would like to go to see the show with her.'

'I hope you said yes,' Tilly intercepted, gesturing with her hands and arms in a theatrical manner as she stated, 'The show is fabulous, and the audience dress for the occasion; you should see them in their lovely basques and their silky or fishnet stockings, and their make-up - it's outstanding.'

'That's disgraceful, dressing like that in public,' sneered Fairbanks. 'What were the men wearing?'

'I'm talking about the men, ' Tilly scoffed, and then turning to Shelly asked, 'Well, did you say yes? Did you go to the show?'

'I said yes. I was so pleased she had asked me to go with

her; she was really nice, and I remembered someone telling me about "The Rocky Horror Show". It sounded like great fun. We were talking about going in fancy dress; not basques, but something gothic.

'And just then, while we were talking, I heard some of the girls from the other side of the room. They were shouting across at us, and one of them yelled, "Oh look, the ugly duckling has found a drake".

'My friend and I stopped speaking and just looked into each other's eyes. I could see that she was hurt by that remark, but I did not know what to do. I could feel myself shaking. I did not want them making fun of me, so I jumped up and, pointing my finger at my friend, I shouted "Poo, you've farted"; then I ran across to the other side of the room to where all the other girls were, and we all started chanting "smelly arse, smelly arse, smelly arse". We must have shouted it a hundred times and we didn't stop until she burst into tears and ran out of the room.

'As she ran from the room all the girls cackled and pointed. I wanted to go after her and hug her and tell her I was sorry, but I didn't. I just joined in with all the others.'

For a few moments there was silence, whilst Shelly seemed to gaze into blank space.

The silence was broken by Fairbanks. 'So what was the point?' he asked in a demanding manner.

'There was no point,' intercepted Tilly. 'Just girls having a bit of fun.'

'I wish we hadn't done it now. I've regretted it ever since.' As Shelly spoke, she did not look at either one of them; she just stared ahead.

'Well, you did do it, just a bit of harmless fun, and if she couldn't take a joke that's her problem.' As Tilly spoke, she gestured with her palms open.

'A joke, a joke,' said Fairbanks. 'What's funny about calling somebody smelly arse?'

'You don't get it, do you?' replied Tilly in a patronising manner. 'It meant nothing; it was just silly schoolgirl stuff.'

Shelly was still gazing ahead of her. Fairbanks now stood directly in front of her, his face just two inches away from her's, and as he spoke he was pointing his finger up and down at the floor.

'They're supposed to go to school to learn, not shout and swear across the classroom. Bring back the cane, that's what I say, that'll learn them.'

'I don't think corporal punishment should be brought back,' Shelly said.

Shelly believed that any act of violence was wrong, and violence perpetrated in a cold calculated manner by a person in authority such as a school teacher or headmaster had no place in society.

'And why not, ay?' asked Fairbanks in an aggressive tone. 'What's wrong with teaching kids a bit of respect?'

Suddenly Shelly changed from her shy timid nature to being assertive and informative.

'A study on corporal punishment showed that hitting children did not gain their respect; it just instill's in them an instinct to react violently towards anyone that angers them.'

'What a load of codswallop.' Fairbanks now raised his voice. 'The cane didn't do me no 'arm.'

'Didn't do me no 'arm, didn't do me no 'arm,' said Tilly, in the most common Essex girl accent she could manage. 'It didn't learn you to talk proper either, did it?'

CLASS A?

It was the day after the rally and the tears were streaming down her face as Shelly walked across the open space close to her home.

Children were playing, people were exercising their dogs, but they were oblivious to Shelly.

She enjoyed strolling across this field, loved the green open space and embraced the feeling of the sun on her face and the wind in her hair; but she was not enjoying the walk now, not today. The man that offered hope, the one who offered guidance, the person that had all the answers, the one that could show the world could become everyone's paradise, had been arrested.

He had been charged with possessing a large quantity of heroin, with the street value of £250,000.

Shelly had just seen it on national television: it was the

main story on the early evening news.

They were showing pictures of him with his hands cuffed behind his back, surrounded by police officers, some of them armed, as they were putting him into the back of a police van.

The news reporter presenting the programme also stated that, along with the class A drugs, the self-styled Preacher was caught in possession of hardcore pornography, some of which involved juveniles.

Shelly was so upset by this she was physically sick; then, without even thinking about what she was doing, she opened the door of the bungalow in which she lived and began to walk.

Shelly just carried on walking; she felt the whole world was coming to an end.

The 17.15 London to Edinburgh train was now reaching a speed of 120 miles per hour as it hurtled along the track …

FATHER DOESN'T LOVE YOU ANY MORE

'All right, little miss posh tart,' sneered Fairbanks, 'I suppose you had the perfect upbringing.'

'No, not really,' answered Tilly. 'I went to a very good school, which my father paid for. A private girls' school in which elocution was on the curriculum. Or, as you would say ... they learnt us how to talk proper. But my home life was a sham; my parents split up when I was a child.'

A smug look appeared on Fairbanks' face. 'You see, I said it: you women with your divorce, it breaks up homes, and who suffers? I'll tell you who suffers, it's the kids – they're the one's that suffer.'

'You're right, us kids did suffer,' replied Tilly in a matter-of-fact manner. 'But Mother didn't want the divorce; she knew where her bread was buttered. Father was a handsome man; in fact, people said he looked like Sean Connery. He also owned a very successful business, and we lived in a large house with a massive garden. Mother would never have left him. It was Father; he went to live with her best friend Carol.

'Of course, I didn't understand exactly what was happening at the time. All I knew was that my daddy would not be living with us any more.

'I'll never forget the day that Mother broke the news to us. My two sisters and I were in the garden playing "What's the time, Mr. Wolf?", when our Mother called us into the house. I was 7, Caroline was 9 and Catherine the youngest was just 5 years old.'

'It must have been nice having sisters,' said Shelly. 'I would like to have had a brother or sister. When I asked daddy why I was an only child, he just said, "you are worth a multitude of angels". I never understood what he meant, but I knew he was paying me a compliment.'

Tilly did not acknowledge Shelly's statement; she just carried on. 'We went into the lounge. Mother and Father were sat on the sofa; they both looked very straight-faced. Mother said in a soft voice that was almost a whisper, "Daddy is going away and he's never coming back". We immediately burst into floods of tears. I grabbed Father's leg and all I could think to say was "no". Caroline just kept screaming "I want you, I want you", whilst Catherine was sobbing uncontrollably and gasping to catch her breath.'

'That must have been terrible,' said Shelly sympathetically. 'What did your parents do?'

This time Tilly answered Shelly. 'They just sat there, showing no sign of emotion. Then Father just got up and walked out the door without saying a word or even acknowledging us girls in any way, whilst I just screamed for him not to go. I watched through the window as his sky blue Silver Shadow Rolls-Royce pulled away.

'Mother looked at us girls and without any compassion said, "Your father doesn't love you any more". Then she stood up and slowly walked upstairs, leaving us girls sobbing our hearts out.'

Tilly was devastated by her father leaving and, like many children going through the trauma of the breakdown of their parents' marriage, she felt that she was in some way to blame. She sank into a deep depression which was totally extreme and unnatural for a seven-year-old and began to regularly wet her bed, which her mother would scold her for and on some occasions would slap her legs. This carried on for the next fifteen months, during which Tilly's mother would humiliate her by making a point of telling people whilst she was present about her bed-wetting problem and informing them that she now had to be sure that Tilly wore a nappy to bed.

This created even more psychological problems for her; as a result of her mother informing the neighbourhood where they lived of Tilly's bladder problem, when the other children saw her they would chant "Nappy nappy, the baby wears a nappy".

When she was older, Tilly realised that the reason her mother had broken the news to her and her sisters about her father leaving in the way that she did was to get at him, without even caring about the hurt it would cause her and her sisters.

IT'S A JUBILEE

'That's the trouble, there's no family values any more,' remarked Fairbanks, as if he had revealed the answer to why the marriage of Tilly's parents had broken up.

'No, the problem is you men carry what little brains you have inside your trousers,' replied Tilly, with a tint of anger present in her voice.

Shelly, trying to bring calm to the conversation, remarked, 'I suppose I was lucky; my parents were really nice.'

'So what does your dad do?' Fairbanks felt that you could tell a lot about a man by his profession, which was why he asked this question.

Shelly was so proud of her father and his profession that she answered immediately, 'He was a fireman, and in his spare time he ran the local Scout group; my mum ran the

Guides. That's how they met; it was at a large gathering of the Scouts and Guides.'

'One of them Jubilees,' said Fairbanks, nodding his head.

'Jamboree. I think the word you're looking for is jamboree,' said Tilly smugly, enjoying the fact that she could correct this man that she disliked immensely.

How fucking stupid can a woman be, Fairbanks thought, and now he was going to put her straight.

'It's a jubilee, and the reason why they called it a jubilee was that the first time they had one was when a king was having his jubilee year.'

'No, you're mistaken,' said Shelly as politely as she could, so as not to cause any offence. 'They are called jamborees and the first one was in 1920. it was the first ever international jamboree and it was held in Olympia, London.'

'How would you know? You weren't even born,' stated Fairbanks, now feeling rather uptight.

Tilly was enjoying seeing him getting hot and bothered and couldn't resist correcting him even more.

'She wouldn't have needed to have been born to know what year it was. I wasn't born in 1066, but I know that was when the Battle of Hastings took place.'

'By the looks of yer, you were in it,' replied Fairbanks, trying to be as insulting as he possibly could.

There was no reply to this comment. A disdainful face was

pulled by the person it was aimed at, and Shelly pretended not to hear it; she just carried on speaking.

'My parents took me to an international jamboree once. It was brilliant meeting people from all over the world, and we used to go to the national ones regularly. They were great fun. I made lots of good friends, and there was so much to do; everybody was always so nice, that's what I liked about them.'

Tilly did not dislike this vulnerable young girl in any way, but she was beginning to feel a little bit resentful about the way she was talking about her happy family life. Tilly's family life was far from being a happy one: she hated her childhood, and her upbringing, so she could not resist commenting. 'Sounds like an excuse to get plastered to me.'

'Oh no,' answered Shelly, shaking her head, 'my parents didn't drink alcohol.'

'So what was their vice?' asked Tilly playfully. 'Don't tell me, wife-swapping.'

'Please don't make fun of my parents ... I miss them so much,' replied Shelly.

THE ABUSE

An uneasy silence followed, with nobody quite knowing what to say; then Fairbanks remarked, 'You say you miss your parents. What do you mean? Don't you see them any more?'

'We did everything together,' answered Shelly, 'apart from when I was at school or Daddy was working; my parents were so much fun. I haven't seen them since I was fourteen.'

This was exactly the answer Fairbanks wanted: the thought of both their parents being divorced when neither he nor his parents had ever been divorced gave him a feeling of being holier than thou.

He remarked, 'So you're both from broken homes.' Then, pointing at Tilly, he sneered, 'And with your mother being a liberated woman, who looked after you while she went to work?'

'Don,t be silly! Mother never went to work,' replied Tilly, with a touch of resentment in her voice.

'She saw that as beneath her. Father made sure we were provided for financially, and an endless stream of men made sure Mother's needs were satisfied. God only knows how many men Mother had in her bed. But there was one man in particular that seemed to be around a lot more often than the others, and we were told to call him Uncle Giles; he was very tall and was always smartly dressed, and he stunk of after shave. He scared me; he had cold, emotionless eyes, and though he spoke quietly there was always a touch of anger present in his voice.

'I was 11 years old when the abuse started.

'Mother had decided to go out with her friends on what she called one of her ladies' nights, and left him to look after us. That evening we three girls went to our rooms as normal. I was sat up in bed watching the television when my bedroom door opened. He walked in and quietly closed the door behind him, holding the handle down as he did so to avoid making any sound. As he slowly approached my bed he put his forefinger on his lips, gesturing me not to speak.

'He took the top of my quilt and pulled it off the bed, then just dropped it to the floor. He then grabbed my feet and pulled me towards him so that I was laying flat. I lay there terrified as he lifted my white cotton nightshirt up past my waist. I didn't know what he was going to do, but I instinctively knew it would not be nice. I just closed my eyes; it makes me feel sick every time I think of what he did to me.

'It seemed to go on forever; he was hurting me - never, up until that moment, had I felt so much pain and humiliation - the tears were rolling down my face.'

'Why didn't you scream for help?' Shelly asked in a compassionate way.

'I couldn't scream; I was petrified. Besides, only Caroline and Catherine would have heard.'

'Did you call the police?' inquired Fairbanks.

'Did I call the police?' repeated Tilly sarcastically. 'First of all, there was no phone by the side of the bed. Secondly, have you ever heard of an eleven-year-old girl dialling 999 and saying "come quick, I've got a fourteen stone man on top of me"?'

'There's no need to be sarcastic,' retorted Fairbanks, with a touch of anger in his voice. 'I meant, did you call them after.'

'Of course not,' answered Tilly, feeling as if she was being blamed for what had happened.

Even though she was in no way to blame for the abuse she suffered as a child, she always felt that in some way she was responsible, because he chose her, and not Caroline, who was older and much prettier. There were many times when she would wonder what it was she did to encourage him to abuse her. 'He said if I told anyone they would take me away and put me in a home for bad children and that I would never see my sisters again. "Look at me," he said; "look at me, do you understand?" I nodded, then he just turned and left the room quietly and cautiously, so as not to make a sound that Catherine or Caroline could hear.

'I just lay there crying silently to myself for what seemed like hours. Then I heard the front door open and Mother come into the house; they were laughing and joking. It made me feel sick that Mother was happy with him after what he had done to me, and then it suddenly went silent. I could not hear anything any more. I crept halfway down the stairs till I got to the point where I could see into the lounge, and there they were: naked on the fireside sheepskin rug having sex.

'I screamed uncontrollably and burst into tears, whilst simultaneously running back to my room and jumping into my bed. I lay there crying like I'd never cried before. Then the door burst open and my Mother stood there looking over me, with him standing behind her. They had thrown some clothes on before they chased me upstairs. Mother was saying, "It's all right, darling; Uncle Giles wasn't hurting me". And while she was speaking he was stood behind her, looking over her shoulder. His eyes were piercing into me in an intimidating way. She repeated that three times before they left my room to go back and finish what they started. That night I cried myself to sleep. But it did not end there: the abuse carried on and each time I felt more and more violated, because each time he made sure I felt more afraid and each time the abuse was worse than the previous.'

The hatred Tilly felt for this despicable man that her mother had told her she was to call Uncle Giles ate at her like a cancer.

'Did you tell your Mother what he was doing?' Shelly asked compassionately.

'No, I was too afraid,' replied Tilly, shaking her head whilst looking at the floor; 'I felt that if I told anyone I would be punished. I feel sick to the bottom of my stomach every time I think about how I let him get away with it.'

'When did it stop?' Shelly asked.

'One day he was just gone. Mother got tired of him and found herself another shag mate. That's what Caroline and I started to call Mother's boyfriends - her shag mates. The first time Caroline said that word I did not know what it meant; then she explained and we both started laughing and shouting "shag mate, shag mate, shag mate".'

'But did you never tell anybody about the abuse?' asked Shelly.

'When I was seventeen I went to a party at my friend Sarah's house. It was her eighteenth birthday celebration; there was loads of alcohol, we had champagne for starters, then people were taking it in turn to mix different cocktails. I sampled every one of them, and I got a bit drunk; in fact, I got very drunk and I vomited all over her parents' brand new Persian carpet. It was multi-coloured red orange yellow with a hint of green - not the carpet, the sick, ha ha ha! Sarah's Dad drove me home and made me sit with my head out of the window for the whole journey so that I would not be ill in his car. He had a big shiny metallic blue Daimler; it was his pride and joy. When we pulled into the driveway of our house, Sarah's Dad got out of the car and walked around to the passenger side and opened the door for me. As I stepped out, he took my arm and walked me the few steps to the house; he then pressed the button on our brass door bell. Mother opened the door wearing a short silky red housecoat with Chinese writing on it. I noticed the way she smiled and winked at him in a flirtatious way as she thanked him for bringing me home - not bothered that I was so drunk I could barely stand.

'Mother was at home on her own that night: her current shag mate was married with young children; he must have been spending time with his family. So she would have to make do with her battery-operated friend.

'I staggered into the lounge and fell bum first onto a beige leather chair. Mother was sprawled out on the sofa, leaning on one arm and pulling her feet up under her, and looking at me like I was a bad smell. I began telling her about Uncle Giles and immediately she leapt off the sofa and screamed at me to shut up. I shouted back "he did it, he did it", then she slapped my face. I felt the tears well up inside my eyes as she waved her finger at me and said through gritted teeth, "You must never tell those awful lies ever again. We are a respectable family; that sort of thing does not happen. It's only the council estate scum that do that type of thing." I never mentioned a word about it to anyone ever again.

'I'm now sure Mother must have known what was going on at the time; but she never said or did a single thing about it. She was more concerned with her semi-detached suburban middle-class image than she was about her own daughter's.'

'Women like that want locking up,' said Fairbanks with a raised voice.

Tilly carried on speaking. 'I had to get away and as soon as the opportunity to leave arose I jumped at it; even though I needed Mother, I despised her. Oh yes, we had a lovely house and nice clothes and all the material things we wanted: paid for by Daddy. But with Mother us girls always came second, to whoever or whatever she was preoccupied with at the time.

'We went to America, my friend Mandy and I. I got a job waiting at tables in a restaurant; it was like an upmarket steakhouse. The furniture and the decor were very plush, the seats were covered with deep red velvety material, and in the middle there was a big round pit with small alligators in. That was the name of the restaurant: *Alligators*.

It was while I was working there that I met one of the other waitresses, Noel. She was the first friend I made in America.'

Noel was very petite; she had short spiky hair and was quite pretty in a sort of boyish kind of way. The two young women were instantly attracted to each other; of course, it was not difficult to spark up a conversation when they were working together. Then one evening after the restaurant had closed and they were clearing the remaining wine glasses from the tables, Noel mentioned to Tilly that there was a late-night movie showing at the local cinema and asked her if she would like to go along with her to see it. Tilly did not need to be asked twice; she immediately answered yes she would love to go. As they sat in the cinema, Noel took Tilly's left hand in her right and held it gently; she felt a tingling sensation throughout her body, as this to her confirmed that this was a real date, not just two girls going to see a film together. As the film ended and as the front of house lights went up, and the audience stood up to leave, Noel looked at Tilly and, raising one eyebrow, asked, 'Coffee?' Tilly did not answer; she just nodded her head and smiled in a most agreeable way. As they walked along the sidewalk in the nice warm summer night air towards Noel's apartment, with neither one of them saying a word, Tilly was excited at the thought of what was to come. For as long as she could remember she had always felt a physical attraction towards girls, but had never had a sexual encounter with another woman before.

They reached the apartment block, then walked through the lobby to the elevator. There was nobody about as it was now 3.15am. The lift doors opened; they stepped in, and as they did so, Noel pushed the button marked 4 and as the door closed and the elevator ascended towards the fourth floor she pulled Tilly towards her and gently kissed her on the lips. Tilly responded and very soon their mouths were locked with their lips slightly parted and their tongues massaging the insides of each other's mouths. They heard a ping as the elevator doors opened. Hanging on to each other as if their lives depended on it, Noel led Tilly to a dark brown door marked with the number *27* with two brass numbers. She reached into her pocket and took out the key, and, as she opened the door, walked through, pulling Tilly behind her, and led her past the bathroom which was on their right and into the bedroom, which, despite the fact that it was tiny, had a large double bed which took up eighty percent of the floor space. Noel slowly undressed Tilly, beginning with her burgundy coloured blouse, which she slowly unbuttoned from the top down; then, pulling it past her shoulders, she allowed it to slip to the floor. As she put her hands behind Tilly's back to unhook her bra strap, they once again locked mouths, before dropping the bra to the floor.

Noel knelt before her and, as she slipped the black knee-length skirt down past her legs, noticed that Tilly was not wearing any garments beneath.

Tilly just stood there as Noel, kneeling before her, marvelled at her naked body. As she stood up, Tilly lay on the bed, looking up at Noel and feeling aroused in anticipation of what was about to happen next.

Noel hurriedly undressed herself: she was wearing similar clothes to Tilly, as the burgundy blouse and black knee-length skirt were the uniform worn by the waitresses at *Alligators*. When she was naked, she laid besides Tilly and gently kissed her on the lips, then slowly worked her way down the voluptuous body till she reached her vagina. She began to manipulate her clitoris with her tongue until she felt Tilly's entire body shudder, and heard her let out an ecstatic cry as she reached a climax.

That was the beginning of their relationship. It was a stormy one, with Noel wanting to announce that they were a couple to all of her family, friends and work colleagues. Tilly would not hear of it.

'If Mandy found out and the word got back to England, it would cause me problems with my Mother; she would not understand' was the answer Tilly would give whenever the subject arose, and as Tilly would not have it anyway other than her way, their relationship stayed in the closet, despite the fact that it carried on until Tilly returned to England.

Fairbanks was shaking his head as Tilly began explaining her relationship with Noel.

'We started going out with each other, like a proper couple; it was a real novelty for me as I had never had an intimate relationship with a girl before, although I was always attracted to girls. Even at school I would look at the other girls in the shower and I would …'

Fairbanks interrupted. 'That's disgusting! You mean you would ogle other girls while they were having a shower?'

'Yes I would, and I would admire their beautiful bodies, and whilst I was doing so I would hope they admired mine too.'

'So you're a dyke.'

Tilly replied sarcastically, 'Good bit of detective work there, Fairbanks. Yes, I'm a dyke, a muff diver, a rug muncher, a tuppence licker and any other derogatory name you wish to call me, you stupid old bigot.'

He folded his arms across his chest in a sign of rejection and muttered, 'Well, at least I'm not a pervert like you.' Then, gazing at her in a bewildered way, he asked, 'And how do you know my name?'

For a few moments there was silence. She did not know his name; she had never met him before, and if she were given the choice she would have chosen not to have any liaison with him whatsoever, but she knew his name. They sat there looking at each other in an inquisitive way.

Shelly broke the silence when she spoke up in defence of Tilly. 'I don't think it's perverted to be attracted to somebody of the same sex as you. I was attracted to a girl once,. I don't know why. I'm not gay or anything like that. I just sort of liked her; it was the girl I was telling you about - you know, the one at school. Han …'

Fairbanks did not allow her to finish. 'Well, if you're attracted to another girl, it's not right; your parents should have taught you that.'

THOSE HIDEOUS MASKS

'My parents taught me lots, and everything they taught me was good. I was fortunate to have had such a lovely Mother and Father,' stated Shelly affectionately.

'You always talk about your parents in the past tense,' observed Tilly.

'I haven't seen them since I was fourteen. One evening my parents and I were at home having dinner, when suddenly we heard an awful noise outside. We got up and looked out through the lounge window and we saw that there was a group of lads outside our house; there was about six or seven of them, and they were wearing these clown masks, and they were shouting and swearing. One of them had a spray can and he was putting graffiti on all of the cars.

'The rest of them had baseball bats and pool cues in their hands and they were bashing them onto the cars. We had a red Ford Sierra estate and I could see they had smashed the windscreen and were trying to completely wreck it.

'My dad wanted to go outside to stop them. He ran to the door, but before he could open it, Mum grabbed him and shouted, "Don't go out there; let's call the police".

'Mum dialled 999. I saw the way her hands were shaking and there were tears welling up in her eyes and then she got angry with the person on the phone and slammed it down, then looked at my father and said, "They say it is not an emergency, but they will send a car when one is available".

'Then a brick came through our window. It landed at my feet, and a piece of broken glass caught me on the side of my face.

'Dad went charging out of the door. Mum went running after him, shouting "No, John, no".

'I followed them, but I did not go outside. I stood in the doorway of our house. I was frozen with fear; it was like it was not happening for real, almost as if I was watching it on the TV.

'My parents were knocked to the floor, then the lads started kicking and stamping on them like they were rag dolls. It seemed to go on forever, but I never heard anything. I just couldn't take my eyes off those hideous masks: they had pink hair, a red nose and a mouth that had a smile painted on, only they were not smiling - they looked angry, like they wanted to kill.

'Then suddenly they stopped and started walking away. Then one turned back, he took his mask off, and walked towards me. Then, as he was poking me in the chest, he shouted, 'You're next, bitch!"; then he punched me in the face. I fell back and hit my head on the floor. It really hurt and my mouth was bleeding. One of our neighbours called for an ambulance, and I was taken to hospital, and after the doctor examined me I was taken to one of the wards for observation. I kept asking to see my Mum and Dad. Then in the morning a lady came to see me; she told me my parents had passed away.

'At first I didn't believe it. I just kept saying, "No, there's been a mistake", and then I started to cry. I cried all day.'

'Then what happened?' asked Fairbanks.

'I went to live with my grandparents.'

'No, how long did they get?'

'What do you mean?' Shelly did not understand his question.

Fairbanks was getting irritated. 'The thugs: did they all get convicted? What was their sentence?'

'Oh no,' Shelly replied, 'I spent a lot of time with the police; they were asking me lots of questions. They seemed really nice, and I told them the names of the boys that did it.'

'But you only saw one of their faces. How could you know the names of all of them?' Instinctively, Fairbanks was questioning Shelly as a police officer would.

'Everybody knew who they were,' replied Shelly, 'they were always causing trouble, and they wore those horrible masks to frighten people.'

'So did the police arrest them? Did they go to court?' Tilly asked.

'No. The police made lots of enquiries, and then after about two months they told us they didn't have enough evidence to prosecute.'

'That didn't happen in my day,' stated Fairbanks assertively. 'If someone was guilty, we made sure they were guilty. You must have been a bad witness.'

'Oh shut up, will you!' Tilly glared at Fairbanks sternly. 'But, Shelly, the one who punched you, you must have got a clear look at him; did you know his name?'

'Yes, I told the police. I wasn't a bad witness. I told them exactly what happened, and when I told them the one that punched me was Dan Collier, they just sort of looked at each other, but they didn't say anything.'

'And yet, despite the fact that you got a clear vision of one of them and you gave the police his name, they got off scot free. That is outrageous,' stated Tilly.

'That's the trouble these days: the law favours the guilty.

It would not happen in my day. Oh no, they wouldn't have got away with it; we would've made sure of that.' Fairbanks pointed at his chest as he made this statement.

'Are you a policeman?' asked Shelly.

'Detective sergeant, 25 years in the job, retired now on full pension and I got decorated: the George Cross. ... The problem is, no-one respects the police any more; in my day people looked up to us - now they call them names like pig and filth.'

Sensing that Shelly was getting upset, Tilly tried to reassure her. 'The problem is there are so many loopholes in the law now, that unless they have an airtight case, the police cannot prosecute. I'm sure the police would have done everything they could to bring the perpetrators to justice.'

'His father was a policeman,' said Shelly.

'Who's father?'

'Dan Collier. His father was a policeman.'

'That's not right, that's not right. There is no way he was a copper's son.' Fairbanks always jumped to the defence of the police without ever questioning whether or not the comment made about them was correct; as far as he was concerned, the police were always right.

'You're lying; you've probably made the whole thing up.' He pointed at Shelly in an accusing way.

'I am not lying.' Shelly now had tears welling up in her

eyes. 'They kicked and battered my parents to death, and you let them get away with it, you covered it up.'

'I have never covered anything up; and even if you are telling the truth, I have never heard of you or your parents before.'

'I don't think she's talking about you personally,' intercepted Tilly. 'I think she's talking about the police force in general.'

The conversation was becoming very heated. Tilly's attempt to calm things down a little had backfired, due to the fact that Fairbanks was full of contempt for any woman that had an opinion of her own, and would never accept any criticism of the police. 'The police do not cover up things,' Fairbanks yelled.

Shelly retaliated. 'So what about the school teacher that was murdered in Southall?'

'A school teacher murdered in Southall; that's news to me,' he answered defensively.

Shelly glared at him in a manner that was totally out of character. 'It's not new. It happened quite a while ago.'

'I haven't a clue what you're talking about, you silly little girl.'

'You know exactly what I'm talking about,' said Shelly accusingly. 'In 1979 a teacher was …'

Fairbanks did not allow her to finish. '1979? What would you know about 1979? You weren't even born.'

'I wasn't born in 1066, but I also know about the battle of Hastings, and I know that in 1979 you killed a teacher when you hit him over the head.'

'I was nowhere near Southall town hall in 1979 and he was not hit with a truncheon, he was hit with a ...'

Fairbanks stopped yelling as quickly as he had started. It went silent, with the three of them just staring at each other. Shelly was shaking with rage and tears were rolling down her cheeks. Never before had she ever got so angry with another person, and had always avoided angry confrontations, preferring to turn the other cheek; unpleasantness was something she had always avoided.

Now she spoke in a more controlled manner as she looked Fairbanks straight in the eye and stated, 'I never said anything about the town hall, or what he was hit with.'

Again, there was an uncomfortable silence. Eyes were staring at Fairbanks. He broke the silence by stating, 'I don't know anything about that case. I retired in '62. I only know what I read in the papers, but that's all I know.'

'You mean you don't know he was killed by policemen in the same way as my parents were killed, and that there were witnesses, both police and civilians, and the whole thing was covered up?'

'You said your parents were killed by thugs.'

'They were killed by thugs. The difference is, the thugs that killed my parents wore clown masks, whereas the thugs that killed the teacher wore blue uniforms, and ten years later paid the victim's brother an undisclosed amount of money to let things lie and not push for an independent inquiry.'

THE UNOFFICIAL CODE

Once again there was silence. Fairbanks was not used to anyone correcting him, let alone a little snip of a girl, and yet he could not think of a single word to say. She was right: a school teacher had been killed in Southall and the person or persons responsible had got away with it, despite the fact that there were a dozen or so witnesses, both police and civilian; but there was an unofficial code that you would not find in any instruction manual, a code that any police officer serving or retired would dare not break.

You never grassed on your own.

The silence was broken by Tilly. 'Why would the police do that? Why would they cover up the truth?'

It was now Shelly that pointed at Fairbanks. 'Because they didn't want anybody knowing the truth, because the one thing the police don't like is the TRUTH.'

'I don't know nothing about that. I told you, I retired in '62.'

Tilly commented, 'You retired in 1962? You don't look old enough.'

'Well, thank you; you've finally said something nice to me.'

'No, seriously, if you retired in '62, you must have been very young.'

Fairbanks now stood upright, shoulders back, arms to his side. The one thing he loved to do was talk about his years in the police force.

'I joined when I was twenty; as I told you, twenty-five years in the job, then I retired.'

'Maths was never my strongest subject, but if you were forty-five in 1962, that makes you eighty-two.'

'It didn't take you long to stop being nice, did it? If you must know, I'm …'

'Ninety-five,' Shelly interrupted.

'What?' Both Tilly and Fairbanks were looking at Shelly with total bemusement. 'Ninety-five. I got a G.C.S.E in maths: if you were forty-five in 1962, then you would be ninety-five now.'

'As I said, maths was not my strongest subject. I only managed to get as far as O level, but I don't need that to work out if a man was forty-five in 1962 he would be eighty-two now.' Tilly gestured towards Fairbanks with an open palm, as if introducing him on to a stage.

'I am not eighty-two and I'm certainly not ninety-five. I am …'

'Talking bullshit!' Tilly intercepted.

'What?'

'Talking bullshit. You never retired from the police force in 1962, if you were ever in the police force at all.'

'Oh yeh, well look at that then.' Fairbanks reached into his inside jacket pocket and took out an old black and white photograph and thrust it under Tilly's nose. 'Who's that in the picture, ay? … Me - and you see that medal on my chest, the George Cross, do you know that is the highest medal for gallantry that any man not serving in the armed forces can receive. Oh yes, you knock the police and criticise them all the time, but you're quite happy for us to take a bullet for you.'

Tilly pushed Fairbanks' hand away from her face. 'Take a bullet. … That.s going a bit far.'

'No, it's not going a bit far. Do you know how many policemen have been killed in the line of duty? No, you don't; and the reason why, is because you don't care.'

HE BLEW HIS FUCKING HEAD OFF

'How many policemen have been killed on duty?' asked Shelly.

'I don't know, but I know I got shot at,' Fairbanks answered, pointing proudly towards his shoulder.

'So how did that happen?'

'I was on duty, working the late shift, and about half-past eight that evening we got a call there was a robbery in progress: two suspects on the roof of a warehouse. Well, I was the first one up there. Oh! Yes! I never worried about the danger to myself; it was always the others I was bothered about. That's why they gave me the George Cross.

'He tried to get away, but I grabbed him - you know, the retarded one - well he stood there frozen stiff. I shouted in his ear, "Police, you're under arrest", then gave him a gentle punch in the stomach so he knew I would stand for no mucking about. Then the other little bastard shot me right in the shoulder. Well, if I hadn't been so tough it might have made me let go, but I held on to the retard – that's why they gave me the George Cross.

'Well, it was like bedlam on that roof. No one really knew what was going on. There was lots of shouting, sirens blaring and loads of other coppers arriving on the scene and all the while the little bastard with the gun was firing bullets all over the place, but I held on to the other one. He knew not to fuck about with me - that's why they gave me the George Cross.

'Well, the armed lads turned up. They didn't have a clue what was going on. They just kept screaming, "Stop, police; stop, police". Then a door burst open and a bullet hit him in the head. He went down like a sack of shit; not slowly like they do in them poxy cowboy films - oh no, he hit the deck straight away. Do you know what it's like to see one of your workmates lying on the floor with half his fucking head blown off?'

Neither one of the women answered. They could tell that Fairbanks did not want an answer. They had discovered that he likes to ask questions for effect, but does not want answers, as the only opinion he values is his own. Fairbanks carried on.

'When the one with the gun realised we had him trapped and there was no way he could escape, he jumped off the roof, right onto a greenhouse. He weren't going nowhere, he weren't capable of moving: broken bones and smothered in blood. Serves the little bastard right.

'Me and two others dragged the retard downstairs and slung him in the back of the wagon.' Fairbanks and his colleagues had agreed not to mention the fact that two of the police officers had grabbed the one with the gun and threw him off the roof. Their story was that he jumped.

Much to the annoyance of Fairbanks, Shelly interrupted. 'That must have been dreadful. I remember we studied that case in college. He was educationally sub-normal - you know, the one you called a retard - he had the mental age of an eleven-year-old; his twin brother died at birth, and then when he was four years old he fell off a lorry he was playing on, which brought about an epileptic seizure. The doctors said he would never be the same again. Such a tragic life.'

'Tragic, tragic.' The rage was now showing in Fairbanks' voice as he once again took a twisted sense of pleasure in showing his aggressive side. He jumped to his feet and stood as close to her as he could without actually standing on her, then, looking down at her, he continued.

'I'll tell you what, tragic is telling a copper's wife that her husband has been killed in the line of duty, then having to explain how, because in between the crying and the screaming she keeps saying, "What happened, what happened?". Have you had to tell anyone how her husband died?'

He paused for a few seconds, not because he wanted an answer but in order to intimidate as much as he could the now very frightened young lady.

Shelly stood there, frozen on the spot.

'Then you don't know what tragic is. And what about the child having to grow up without a father? In them days kids actually knew who their fathers were; there was none of all that women bringing different men home from the pub every night in them days. No, once a woman was married she stayed married, for better or worse. How would you like to have to explain to your child that daddy`s never coming home again?'

TOMMY

'Tommy, I've got a little parcel here for you; something to take home to your mum.'

Tommy stopped sweeping and looked up towards Ted, who was standing behind his fruit and veg stall on the corner of the street market.

For the past two years eighteen-year-old Thomas Taylor had been working for the local council sweeping the streets in the area in which he lived, but his favourite street was Surrey Street, with its lively character, full of market stalls and friendly jovial banter coming from the local traders.

The traders always made a fuss of Tommy, and loved him for his pleasant personality and his readiness to do more than his job entailed. Any time Tommy saw an elderly person struggling with heavy shopping he would stop what he was doing, and carry the shopping to that person's home; on reaching the destination, if any of the people that Tommy had assisted offered him any financial reward, he would refuse to take it and would answer, 'No thank you, I have all the money I need.'

It was 1952 and only the very wealthy people had motor cars, so people would shop locally.

If Tommy fell behind with his work as a result of his good deeds, he would carry on working to make up for it. He walked over to Ted's fruit and veg stall. Ted patted Tommy on the shoulder as he said, 'I'm afraid I've made a bit more mess today than I normally make. Can you take care of it for me?'

'Yes, Mister Cooper,' Tommy replied.

'And don't call me mister,' Ted retorted with a smile on his face. 'You're one of us lads now. I keep telling you to call me Ted; and when you've finished there's a box of veg there to take home to your mum, and I've put in a couple of juicy red apples for your beautiful sister Violet.'

'Thank you, Ted,' Tommy replied. 'Violet loves apples.'

'Tommy, can you give us a hand with this?' called Dave from the fabric stall, and Tommy hurried over to see how he could help.

'Do you know his sister Violet absolutely adores him,' Mrs Wilson said to Ted as she approached his stall to buy her vegetables for the weekend. 'Whenever I see her she never talks about anything else, always telling me how helpful he is around the house, and you know he tells his mum and his sister he loves them every day, and despite the fact that lad got picked on at school for being a bit backward, he ain't got a bad bone in his body, bless his little heart. It's a pity all the young lads around here ain't like him.'

The young lad that Detective Sergeant Fairbanks chose to refer to as the retard was known and loved by everyone else as Tommy.

HOMO SAPIENS

The two women slowly shook their heads from side to side. With Fairbanks now feeling satisfied that his attempt to intimidate the women had succeeded, he sat back down slowly.

There was an uneasy silence; the three of them just sat with their arms folded across their chests, gazing into blank space, reminiscing about some of the tragic events that had occurred in their lives. It was Tilly that broke the silence.

'I know how that feels. It's not nice; and, as I told you, I can still remember clearly being told my father was leaving and not coming back.'

'That must have been terrible,' Shelly said sympathetically.

'I can understand why you went to America when you were old enough. It must have made a nice change. How long were you there for?'

'A few years, and when I got back from America it was a real culture shock: all my old school friends had settled down, every single one of them had boyfriends, a couple of them even had engagement rings on their fingers. I thought it was pathetic. I wanted to say, "What are you doing with these men? These pathetic little boys". But I couldn.t. Do you know when I was your age how difficult it was to come out and say, "Look, I am gay"? Of course not, how could you know? Nowadays, when a girl comes out they throw a party for her, buy her presents. It was not like that when I was your age. If I had opened up, my friends would have turned away from me, my mother would have disowned me; though, for the amount of attention she showed me, I doubt that I would have noticed any difference.'

'But that's not right,' said Shelly. 'There's nothing wrong with loving somebody, regardless of whether that person is a man or a woman.'

Fairbanks jumped to his feet. 'No, there's nothing wrong with a man loving a woman, or a woman loving a man, but a woman loving a woman? Well, that's not right; it goes against nature.'

'But love is the most natural thing there is,' said Shelly.

'Only when it's between a man and a woman,' Fairbanks stated. 'We didn't have none of those *homo sapiens* in my day.'

Even though Shelly was afraid of Fairbanks, she could not resist the urge to correct him.

'Don't you mean homosexuals? *Homo sapien* just simply means human being.'

'*Homo sapiens*, homosexuals - it doesn't matter what you call them.' Then, pointing his finger at Tilly, he yelled, 'It shouldn't be allowed, and I wouldn't blame your mother if she had disowned you.'

'I don't think you're being very fair.' Shelly leapt to her defence.

'Life's not fair, not one bit fair. I brought my son up to understand that, and if your father brought you up proper, you'd understand that.'

'Don't speak about my father like that; my father was a good man.'

Tilly turned to Fairbanks and, looking at him in a disgusted way, asked, 'So what would you do? If your son told you he was gay, would you turn your back on him?'

'It wouldn't happen,' he replied with a misplaced sense of pride. 'My son's a real man with a real career: he's a parking regulatory officer.'

'A traffic warden!' Tilly laughed in a mocking way.

TREVOR THE TRAFFIC

To the majority of people a Traffic Warden is as low down the food chain as a cockroach or a sewer rat. In Tilly's eyes, anybody that does an unskilled low-paid job is low down, but a traffic warden?!

She carried on her mocking laugh until Fairbanks interrupted in his son's defence. 'You know, it's men like my son that keep this country straight, stop it from going under, by keeping the low lifes in order.'

Tilly replied to this comment in a belittling tone of voice. 'Handing out parking tickets.'

'By making them obey the law and punishing those that don't. And he believes in the survival of our race. You know, my son makes a donation to the sperm bank every week.'

Whilst making a rude gesture with her right hand, Tilly commented, 'So, he takes after his father.'

The only thing that Fairbanks' son had ever done that made him proud was becoming a traffic warden, because now at least Gary had a sense of purpose. There was no way he was going to discuss the anger and the disappointment he felt when his only child failed his entrance exam to join the police force. In a fit of rage when he heard about Gary failing, he grabbed him by the throat and, pinning him against the wall, screamed, 'Any idiot could pass the entrance exam1.

But young Gary Fairbanks was not any idiot: he was quite unique. At school he was bottom of the class in every subject. 'There's no hope for you,' his form teacher would say.

How much Gary wished that one day Mr. Baker his teacher would see him in his uniform, so that he could prove that he had made something of his life.

Gary really hated his school days: the teachers would scold him for his poor exam results, and the other kids would bully him for being what they called a freak.

It was while he was employed as a traffic warden that he made his first ever friend.

Trevor the Traffic was the name he gave to his friend, on account of him also being a traffic warden, and his name being Trevor. Gary felt quite proud of himself for thinking up such a witty name, and Trevor liked it because it had the same ring to it as Billy the Kid and Roy of the Rovers.

Up until then the only nicknames Trevor had were as a result of his surname being Greengrass and the fact that he would go to the Headmaster to report on any of the other kids that had done something they shouldn't. 'Fat grass', 'Smelly grass', 'Shit arse' were among the nicknames that he had at school, and, like Gary, he hated school. But now he was a man, and due to his mother's position as local councillor, he now had a job of which he was proud, and he had a real friend - his life could not be better. So the dynamic duo, as they liked to call themselves, became inseparable.

Their favourite days to go on patrol, as they liked to call it, were bank holidays, when most people thought that Sunday restrictions applied. They could issue four times as many tickets on those days as they could on a normal day.

Trevor was the only person that understood why Gary was upset with his mother for shouting at him for giving her a parking ticket.

'You were on a meter and hadn't paid,' he said in his defence.

'I drove over there to give you your sandwiches, you stupid little bastard, and whilst I was walking around looking for you, you stuck a ticket on my car,' she screamed.

Gary sobbed. He really was upset, because up until that

point the only person he knew apart from Trevor that had never shouted at him or insulted him in any way had been his mother.

'If your Mum doesn't understand the importance of the job we do, then she is not intellectually your equal,' stated Trevor, with one arm around the sobbing Gary's shoulders, as they sat in Trevor's room.

Trevor lived with his mother, Councillor Greengrass, a widow, as Trevor's father, a respected surgeon in his field, had passed away when he was a child, leaving Councillor Greengrass financially stable and with a five-year-old son.

Although she had doted on her son, she found him a disappointment, not just because of his failure academically, but also his inability to fit into society.

So Councillor Greengrass was delighted when he found himself a friend, and gave permission for Gary to stay at her house whenever he wished.

The house had eighteen rooms, not counting the bathrooms, so there was plenty of space.

Due to Gary's mother's unreasonable behaviour and a lack of understanding as to the importance of the profession he was in, Gary now spent more time at Trevor's house, and the dynamic duo became even closer; until the day Trevor's mother broke the news to him that they were going to Norfolk to spend a week's holiday with her sister and that, despite his pleading, Gary would not be allowed to accompany them.

Those seven days seemed like an eternity to Gary. When not out patrolling the streets, he just sat in his room, staring at his *Star Trek* posters; for the first time in his life he knew how it felt to miss someone. The evening before Trevor the Traffic was due back from Norfolk, Gary was as excited as a five-year-old on Christmas Eve; but then the devastating news was broken to him that his friend would not be returning the next day or any day.

In the police interview room sat a very nervous Trevor. 'I was walking across the field when all of a sudden I needed to go to the toilet and that was why my trousers and pants were down,' he stated defensively. But when he could not explain how his penis came to be wedged between the sheep's buttocks, his solicitor suggested that he should enter a guilty plea.

Trevor received a six-month suspended jail sentence and ordered to pay costs.

On the third page of a national newspaper, next to a photo of a young model wearing just a skimpy pair of briefs, with the title of 'Kirsty, age 20, from Merseyside', who's wisdom for the day was, 'I think people that break the speed limit need to learn to drive more slower', was the headline

COUNCILLOR GREENGRASS SON
CAUGHT UP THE SHEEP'S A***E

It was suggested that, as a result of this adverse publicity, Councillor Greengrass should resign from her position, which she did without fuss, to avoid any further embarrassment.

'It could have been worse,' stated her friend. 'If it had not been for that photograph being taken by the paparazzi of a back-bench M.P. with an eighteen-year-old rent boy on Clapham Common, you would have been on the front page.'

This was of no consolation to a woman who had ambitions to stand for Parliament and who felt a tingly sensation every time she was introduced as councillor. Sadly, that would happen no more.

So Mrs Greengrass decided to go back to using her maiden name, and to move as far away as possible to start a new life. Out of a sense of maternal duty, she took along her son Trevor, and forebad him to tell anyone where they were living, as it was important for them to start over again. And, of course, he was not allowed anywhere near sheep. Mrs Greengrass never ate lamb again.

And Gary never saw or heard from his friend ever again.

After a long period of mourning, Gary spent his time patrolling the streets, watching old episodes of *Star Trek*, and making donations to the sperm bank. He never made another friend.

JUSTICE

'You have no idea what really goes on, do you? You think it's like in the pictures: a copper says to someone you're nicked and that's the end of it. Well, I tell you what, that is only the start. When we got back to the station after my mate got shot, it was like Bedlam: no-one knew what was going on, everybody was just shouting and screaming. The guv'nor called a meeting, and told us all to calm down, put our heads together, then write our reports.

Then we found out the little bastard with the gun was only sixteen. A copper got killed because he was on the roof spraying bullets all over the place, but would he swing for it? No, he wouldn't. Just a few years' bird, then he would be free - the low-life scumbag would be free.

'We weren't standing for it. One of our own got shot

dead, killed, murdered, whatever you want to call it, and somebody was going to pay.

'I interviewed the retard; it was like talking to a kid. "I was just following George; we weren't going to do nothing" was all he could say. A policeman is dead, shot in the head as a result of you not doing nothing.'

Fairbanks paused, which Shelly took as an opportunity to voice her observation. 'The poor thing. He must have been terrified, with you shouting at him like that.'

This irritated Fairbanks, who had no sympathy for any person partaking in any crime. 'A copper was lying in the morgue. What would you expect me to do: give him a fucking kiss?'

'But he didn't shoot your friend. you said that yourself. You were holding on to him at the time; it was the other lad who …'

'Was only sixteen.' Fairbanks did not give her a chance to finish the sentence; he just yelled in her ear. He was now shaking with rage and wanted to show it, and finished his outburst with, 'And according to the law he could not be hung. An eye for an eye, a tooth for a tooth; we wanted justice.'

Anger is a powerful, destructive emotion. And in the police station that day the anger was rife. One of their colleagues, a man they saw in the corridors and in the factory canteen on a daily basis (factory is the policemen's term for the police station) had been killed, and even though the death sentence for murder was mandatory, it was looking like nobody was going to stand face-to-face with the hangman's noose.

'Me and my colleagues, we all just sat there round a table; gutted we were, then someone said, "Hold on, there was a case about twenty years ago. A copper got killed; same thing, there was two of them, only one shot him, only one had a gun, but they both swung for it." We just looked at each other for a minute. No-one said a word. Carry on, I told him, carry on. Well, he said the arresting officers just said one of them shouted "Let him have it", and then the other one fired the gun. They both got guilty for murder, they both swung, job done.

'So that was that. All I had to say was that, when I was holding him, he shouted "Let him have it".'

'But did he say that? Did he say "Let him have it"?' asked Shelly in as soft a tone of voice she possibly could, so as not to infuriate him any further.

'What he said and what he didn't say ain't the point. The point is, we wanted justice and we were gunna make sure we got it.' Fairbanks was pointing his forefinger towards the ground as he said it.

It has become common practice among the police to say a person standing accused of a crime had said something whilst under arrest, after being cautioned, that he or she didn't say, in order to secure a conviction. After all, who are the jury or magistrates going to believe? The person standing in the dock or the arresting police officer?

'But surely telling lies is not the way to get justice,' Shelly said.

'So how do you think the guilty get innocent verdicts, ay?

They don't get them by telling the truth, Oh no, they lie; they lie right through their teeth. Every day some no good low-life scumbag gets a not guilty, because the jury believed his fucking lies.'

Most things angered Fairbanks, but nothing angered him more than when he saw someone he knew he had bang to rights, and was as guilty as sin, get a not guilty verdict.

'But if you lie as well, does that not make you as bad as them?'

'As bad as them, as bad as them! Don't you dare compare me to the scum I put away. You have no idea what goes on, you stupid little bitch.'

Hearing Fairbanks speak to a young woman in that tone inflamed Tilly, coupled with the fact that she had a deep resentment of men, due to her father leaving and the abuse she suffered at the hands of Uncle Giles. 'That's enough,' she screamed at him, 'there is no need to speak to her like that.'

'I was only trying to say I think it's wrong to tell lies about somebody,' added Shelly defensively.

'Oh! Darling, you are so naive; people lie in order to achieve their goals all the time,' said Tilly.

'I lied when I said my school friend farted and now I feel sick every time I think about it,' Shelly replied.

Tilly put her hand on Shelly's and, giving it a gentle comforting squeeze, said, 'Oh, come on, that was no big deal. As I said earlier, it was just schoolgirl stuff. How do you think I feel: my whole life has been a lie, but the one I regret the most is the one I told about my husband.'

Shelly raised her eyebrows in a manner that indicated surprise. 'Your husband. ... But I thought you were …'

'A lesbian ...' Tilly intercepted. 'Yes, as I told you, I'm a lesbian, but as I also said I could not come out, so I decided to conform. I kissed a lot of frogs, then I met a nice guy and we married.'

'And they lived happily ever after,' remarked Fairbanks in the most sarcastic tone he could possibly manage.

Tilly snapped at him. 'No, they did not live happily ever after.'

JULIE

'What happened?' Shelly asked. 'Did it not work out? Did he turn out to be bad?'

'No, he wasn't bad; he was kind, caring, considerate. But how could it possibly work out? You don't need to have the brains of Einstein to figure he wasn't my type. But he just so happened to be the sweetest guy I have ever met. Do you know, he told me he loved me every single day.'

'That's nice,' replied Shelly. 'You know, my grandparents were always telling me they loved me. And they were always saying "I love you" to each other.'

'Your grandparents sound like the perfect couple to me.'

'They were. My granddad use to say, "If you can't think of something nice to say, then say nothing", and "You reap what you sow, because Life is like a curry: what you do today will burn your bum tomorrow" ... I am not quite sure what he meant.'

Tilly nodded and replied, 'Your grandfather was spot on. There is no such thing as a free lunch, and we pay the price for everything we do. Against my better judgement I married a man who doted on me and our daughter, and now I regret it every single day. It was never going to last, I knew all the way along. But when I decided to leave him, I couldn't; it was not …'

Shelly interrupted. 'You have a daughter? ... What's her name?'

'I called her …'

'That should not be allowed,' barked Fairbanks. 'Lesbians having children - there should be a law against it.'

'Anybody is entitled to have children and anybody's entitled to be happily married.'

Neither of the other two acknowledged Shelly's sheepish comment.

'I wanted out of that marriage. It was a sham. I was sick of living a lie. I didn't love him, even though I regularly told him I did. But how could I divorce a man who doted on me and our daughter? I couldn't claim adultery; he never even looked at another woman.'

'Why did you not just leave him?'

'I wanted to. Julie kept telling me too, but I told her to wait. I didn't want to lose my house.'

'Julie? Who's Julie?'

Julie was a police officer in the Hertfordshire Constabulary; she was 5ft 9in tall, medium build and quite plump, but not what you would describe as fat, though she did have a really big bum; and even though she forced a smile most of the time, there was always a look of resentment present in her eyes. She never knew her parents: her mother was unemployed, an alcoholic and also a user of unprescribed drugs, and in order to maintain her habits she sold her body on the streets.

Julie was born in The Sunderland Royal Hospital and as soon as her mother felt well enough she just walked away from the ward without discharging herself or taking her baby with her. The authorities tried to trace her, but found the name she had given was false and the address was a communal squat.

So the life of Julie began in a number of short-term foster homes.

At the age of seven, Rita and Paul adopted her.

Rita and Paul were both in their early thirties. They had met in their late teens whilst they were at university, and had now been very happily married for ten years.

Despite Rita being told she was unable to bear children,

to give a child a loving caring home was their dream and now they could fulfil it. Adopting a child was something Rita and Paul had discussed at great length on many occasions, and it was agreed that Rita would take a break from her career as a dental nurse to be a stay-at-home mum.

Their task was not an easy one. The child they adopted was difficult to manage. They took her to a child psychologist, who explained to them that it was not unusual for a child without a stable background to behave unreasonably, and in time, given the right amount of care and understanding, she would calm down and behave in the correct manner.

Julie did not improve. She would physically attack smaller children both at school and in the street where she lived; at home, if she could not get what she wanted, she would scream, kick Rita and throw objects around the house until her adoptive parents gave in to her.

But it was when she set fire to her bedroom, then told everybody who would listen that Rita did it, that she was handed back to social services.

Rita, with tears pouring from her face, told the distraught Paul, 'Either she goes or our marriage is over, because I just cannot take any more.'

So Julie spent her childhood, when not in a care home, moving from one set of foster parents to another, resenting all the other children she met, hating the parents she never met and never bonding with anyone.

At the age of fourteen she joined a gang of about twenty teenage lads. She was the only girl member, but the lads let her join because she could fight like a boy, and she would grant them sexual favours, which she hated doing, but found it could get her what she wanted; the lads would give her cigarettes as a way of payment.

Julie always wanted to be a boy and cursed God for making her a girl. She always refused to wear anything that she considered to be girlie.

Early one evening, Julie suggested they break into a large warehouse that stored electrical goods, which they did by breaking the lock off with a crowbar. As they were rummaging through the goods to decide what they were going to take with them, they heard two police cars pull up outside. Four policemen came through the door that they had entered through, and as they looked around for a way to escape Julie realised the only way out was the way they came in, but that was blocked by policemen, so she screamed, 'Help, help me, help'. Her quick thinking paid off: the lads got arrested, but not Julie - she was seen as a victim.

At the police station she was comforted by a woman police constable. She felt like a celebrity: she was paid so much personal attention, they got her anything she asked for (apart from cigarettes) when she asked for them.

The W.P.C that was comforting her explained,

"'It is against the law for any person under the age of sixteen to smoke, so therefore we would be breaking the law if we provide you with cigarettes.'

Julie replied by giggling and saying, 'I was only joking. I knew that, and I've never smoked.'

She never mentioned the fact that she had started smoking at the age of twelve.

Whilst she was at the police station she was asked if she would be prepared to make a statement regarding the incident at the warehouse. She replied, 'I really don't want to, but I feel it is my public duty to do so.'

In her statement she said: 'I was walking past the warehouse when four of the lads dragged me inside. They were trying to take my clothes off when, luckily for me, the police arrived. They must have heard me screaming. If they hadn't turned up, who knows what would have happened.'

The lads all got sent to a youth detention centre; Julie received a pat on the back and a financial payment as compensation.

When she reached the age of nineteen, she realised that, with no job, no family or friends to call her own, and no future prospects, the best thing she could do was join the police force. For the first time in her life she felt that she had found her place in society.

'Julie was my partner,' said Tilly. 'She and her husband were in the police force together.'

'You mean you were having an affair with a W.P.C,' said Fairbanks, looking as disgusted as he could.

'We were in love.'

'That should never be allowed. That's what gives the police force a bad name.'

'Do you have any idea what it's like to be in love with someone and not be able to show it openly? To just be able to catch a limited amount of time with them,' said Tilly through gritted teeth.

Of course Fairbanks did not know. He felt that any show of affection was a sign of weakness. He replied, 'A woman shouldn't be in the police force, let alone a lesbian; that's what gives us a bad name.'

Even though Shelly was passive and always avoided any discussion that could lead to a heated argument, certain statements she heard from people made her feel that she should speak up. 'No, what gives you a bad name is killing people then covering it up, and when people call you because they are being terrorised by thugs you do nothing about it because one of the thugs is the son of a policeman. That's what gives you a bad name.'

Poking her in the chest, Fairbanks shouted, 'You know nothing about the police force.'

Tilly ignored the exchange of words between the other two and carried on speaking. 'She had already left her husband and wanted me to tell Stephan it was over between us. But how could I? It was easy for her - she didn't have any children, and her man didn't give two hoots about her; but I had a lovely home. I couldn't just walk away from it all. Then one day Stephan had left for work, and Julie called round, and while we were upstairs I heard Hannah scream. it was the most horrific sound I had ever heard. I rushed downstairs, not even bothering to get dressed. Hannah was lying on the kitchen floor. Her face was covered in blood, and she was screaming the most ear-piercing scream I had ever heard. I shouted to Julie, "Quick, call an ambulance".

' "No," she said. "I will drive us there. It will be quicker." '

Shelly was now very concerned. She asked, 'What happened? Was your daughter seriously hurt?'

'Thankfully, just a broken nose and severe bruising to her face. The doctor said there were no internal injuries, but they felt it best to keep her in the hospital overnight for observation. It seemed she had climbed onto the kitchen worktop and slipped.'

Fairbanks took the opportunity to speak down to

Tilly, which was something he did gleefully. 'If you hadn't neglected her, if you weren't upstairs getting up to disgusting perverted things, it would not have happened. You're to blame, no one else.'

Tilly screamed at him and whilst doing so put her hand over her ears to give emphasis to her answer. 'Oh shut up will you! Do you not think that very thought was not going around my head?'

Fairbanks was now really gloating. He loved the fact that he was getting to Tilly. 'So, come tell us, how did you explain that to your husband?'

'What did you say?' inquired Shelly softly. 'Did you tell him what happened?'

Tilly slowly took her hands away from her ears. She looked at Shelly; she did not scream out in reply to her question, but spoke in a quiet, well-mannered tone.

'No. After that incident we never ever spoke to each other again. Ironically, the last words he said to me as he was leaving for work that day were "I love you", and the last words I said to him were "I love you too". I would never have dreamt at that point that I was never going to see him again, apart from inside a courtroom.'

'A courtroom! Why? Did he want to take your daughter away?' asked Shelly.

'I wouldn't blame him if he did,' Fairbanks sneered.

Tilly chose to ignore his remark and answered Shelly. 'No. But Julie did warn me that he might try. The drive back from the hospital was a silent one; neither one of us said a word. All I could think of was my little girl, and how she was feeling alone in the hospital. We had never spent a whole night apart before. She was the most beautiful being that ever graced the earth; just a couple of days previous we were celebrating her fourth birthday: I can still see the great big beaming smile on her face as she blew out the candles on her birthday cake. And now, due to my negligence, she would be spending the night in a hospital bed.'

'It must have been terrible for you,' Shelly said sympathetically.

Tilly did not answer. She just carried on speaking. 'When we got back to my house, I got out of the car and Julie followed behind. I put the key in the door and, just as I was opening it, she broke the silence. "What are you going to say?" I never replied. I just walked across the hallway and up the flight of stairs to my baby's room and, opening the door, I looked at her little bed and her soft cuddly toys surrounding it and I just burst into tears.'

Shelly may have been sympathetic, but Fairbanks wasn't. In as aggressive a tone as he could muster, he asked, 'So what did you say? Did you tell the truth? Did you say the reason why your daughter had a broken nose and a bruised face was, instead of looking after her like a mother should, you were upstairs getting up to no good with another woman?'

Tilly did not allow him to say any more. She screamed at him. 'How dare you ask me that? How dare you judge me?'

Fairbanks was not going to let go. He waved his finger at her. 'So, did yer tell the truth, did yer?'

'No I didn't. You know I couldn't tell the truth. I was looking for a way to end my marriage. If I told the truth he may have got custody of our daughter; I was not going to let that happen. My head was in a turmoil. I couldn't stop shaking. I was standing in the doorway, looking into my little girl's room, when Julie came up behind me. She put her arm around my shoulder, and then walked me downstairs into the lounge. As she sat me down on the sofa, she looked me straight in the eyes and said,

"People are going to ask questions. You need to get your story straight." I just sat there trembling.'

Although Shelly remained sympathetic, she was becoming confused about Tilly's explanation. 'What did she mean, get your story straight? It was an accident; surely people would understand.'

Tilly did not appear to hear the question; she just carried on speaking, 'Julie picked up the phone and dialled. When a voice on the other end of the line answered, she said, "This is W.P.C Warren"; and then after a brief conversation she turned to me and said, "They will be here shortly to take a statement from you". She told me to say Stephan had lost his temper with Hannah and punched her on the nose before he stormed out.

'I told her I couldn't say that, and besides, who would believe me? He wouldn't hurt a fly. She got very angry. She grabbed hold of my shoulders and, as she squeezed them, in a very stern voice she asked, "Do you want out of your marriage? Do you want to keep your home? And do you want to keep your daughter? Do you?"

'I just nodded my head in agreement. I think at that moment I would have agreed to anything. She told me to say he was prone to violent outbursts and that I was afraid of him.'

THE WHOLE TRUTH

'The lounge door was open when the doorbell rang. I was still on the sofa and I could see the silhouettes through the yellow frosted-glass strips in the oak door. Julie walked to the door and as she opened it the two uniformed policemen standing there removed their hats, while she gestured with her hand for them to come in. As they walked along the hallway towards me, I noticed they were both tall and around forty years old; one of them had two stripes on the arm of his jacket.

When they came into the lounge, Julie suggested they take a seat. As they did so, one of them took a small notepad and pen from his breast pocket; as he did so, he looked at me and asked, "Do you feel able to make a statement at this time?"

'I didn't answer. I just nodded. As I was making the

statement, I was crying and shaking. The picture I painted of Stephan was that he was a violent, bad tempered control freak whom I was afraid of; and whilst I was telling those damning Lies, Julie sat next to me, holding my hand, and a couple of times she said to me, "It's all right, take your time."

'One of the policemen suggested I see a doctor. I just shook my head. When I finished making my statement, Julie said, "It will be all right now. We'll make sure he never hurts you or your little girl ever again."

'Julie walked the policemen down the hallway to the door; they stood there speaking for a few minutes, but I could not make out what they were saying as they were talking in a whisper. When they left, she closed the door behind them, then came down the hallway into the lounge with a great big beaming smile on her face and said, "Well done. I'm proud of you"; then she threw her arms around me and gave me a great big hug.

Fairbanks detested women like Tilly and relished the opportunity to sneer. 'Proud? Proud? You just wasted police time telling lies about an innocent man and you're proud.'

'No, I'm not proud. I've never been so ashamed in my whole life - that's the point. He was arrested and remanded in custody. Of course I'm not proud.'

'Do you mean he was given a prison sentence?' Shelly asked.

'It means he was detained until the trial date,' Fairbanks corrected her, feeling pleased that she had given him the opportunity to do so. Then, pointing his finger at Tilly, he said, 'So you got what you wanted.'

'No, I did not get what I wanted. The whole thing completely spiralled out of control; I just got swept along with it. Fourteen weeks after Stephan was arrested, at eleven o'clock on a Tuesday morning, the case was heard at the local crown court and I went along to give evidence.

'I was waiting outside courtroom two, with Julie holding my hand, and as we sat on the long wooden bench I just kept on saying, "I don't want to do this". Julie said, "You have to give evidence now, otherwise you could be prosecuted for wasting police time. All you need to do is remember what we talked about. Now go in there and give your evidence against him; then it will all be over, and you won't need to worry any more."

'I was looking around to see if Stephan had any character witnesses to speak on his behalf. Everybody that knew him knew he wouldn't hurt a fly. He was popular amongst his fellow volunteers at the Saint John's Ambulance and I was expecting to see some of them there to support him.

'When my name was called, Julie gave my hand a gentle squeeze and wished me luck as I stood up to enter the courtroom. When I walked through the door I felt like a gladiator stepping into the arena of a coliseum; all eyes were looking at me as I sauntered slowly to the witness stand. I put my hand on a bible, then read out loud the words from a card the usher was holding before me: "I swear to tell the truth, the whole truth and nothing but the truth, so help me God."

'I then looked up and saw Stephan sitting in the dock. He looked so alone, so helpless; but I felt no compassion for him. As Julie had explained to me, my marriage was over and I now needed to concentrate on what was best for me and my daughter.

'I was shaking all over as I gave evidence, but it was not as bad as I thought it would be, and then when I had finished and was told I could step down, I felt a sense of satisfaction, similar to how I felt when I passed my driving test.

'When Stephan's barrister called him to give evidence he never moved; he just stayed where he was in the dock and slowly shook his head from side to side. His barrister asked the judge if he could have a moment to speak with his client; he then went over to the dock where Stephan was sitting and was speaking in a whisper for a minute or so, then went back to his place and, addressing the judge, said, "My client has informed me he does not wish to take the stand". He put up no defence at all.

'With my evidence and the police stating that when they

arrested Stephan he said, "She wouldn't stop screaming, so I lost my temper and punched her", he didn't stand a chance. It took the jury just thirty-five minutes to return a guilty verdict. He received a custodial sentence.

'As he was passing sentence, the judge said he was appalled at Stephan's lack of remorse.'

Shelly was now feeling more confused than ever. 'But he hadn't committed any crime; how could he be showing remorse?'

Tilly did not answer; she just carried on speaking. 'I have never seen Julie so happy, she could not stop smiling, and when we got home she went straight to the fridge, took out a bottle of champagne, then she shook it up, popped the cork and said, "We got a result - let's celebrate." That night we got very drunk, then the next morning when I woke up, Julie was not there; she had got out of bed and gone out leaving me asleep. I heard the door open and she came running up the stairs; she was very excited. "Better start packing," she said, "I have booked us a holiday in the Caribbean; we fly from Gatwick on Friday morning." I jumped out of bed and threw my arms around her. I was delighted.'

So they collected Tilly's daughter from the hospital, then contacted an agency and got a live-in Nanny to look after her while they went away for their holiday.

'This is a holiday of a lifetime,' said Julie as their plane was taking off.

Tilly was feeling ecstatic: her husband was out of her life, she had got their home, and with a conviction for a violent attack on their daughter her husband would have no claim to it whatsoever; and now here she was jetting off to the sun with the woman she loved. But Julie had not done any research. The reason why the holiday was such a bargain was the country they were heading for was now in the hurricane season and the hotel they were booked into as part of their package had a history of poor hygiene.

When they reached their hotel, there was a strong gale blowing; the pool furniture had been taken inside, and the hotel residents were crammed inside the lobby, where there was a small cocktail bar in the corner, with a dozen or so people waiting to be served. The one barman serving moved at a snail's pace and showed absolutely no interest whatsoever in the job in which he was gainfully employed. This did not please Tilly, as her idea of a holiday is to be waited on hand and foot; the idea of waiting in a queue for a drink with people that looked like they had come from a council estate, to be served by a barman that did not care whether he served her or not, was not her idea of the perfect holiday hotel.

On day two of the holiday, Tilly contracted salmonella

poisoning: never before had she felt so ill, she was sweating and shaking and she had vomited so much that there was nothing left to fetch up. When she retched, she felt her stomach twisting and tightening; if her head was not down the toilet bowl, her arse was on it.

On the one day that she felt well enough to leave the hotel room, they returned to find their cash, credit cards and passports missing.

What Julie had perceived to be the holiday of a lifetime was, in fact, the holiday from hell.

NIGHTMARES

What is a nightmare? We all have nightmares from time to time.

But how do we define a nightmare? What brings them about?

Films are made about them. Books are written about them. Why the fascination with them?

Tilly sat there, gazing ahead not looking at anything. She broke the silence. 'Since that day in court, my life has been one continuous nightmare.'

Even though Shelly totally disapproved of the false testimony that Tilly made against her husband, she sympathised with her, as she herself could not close her eyes without seeing haunting images.

'I have nightmares all the time. I keep seeing my friend …'

Fairbanks did not allow Shelly to finish her sentence. He stood up and hollered, 'Nightmares! Nightmares! You don't know what nightmares are.'

Shelly had never before had the courage to talk about her nightmares, but now she felt the need to tell the other two. With tears in her eyes, she said, 'I do. I keep having nightmares about my …'

This time Fairbanks interrupted without even acknowledging that she was speaking. With an outstretched arm, he pointed his finger at Tilly and he bawled, 'So you got your story straight and got your husband sent down for a few months.'

'Two years,' was her reply.

'Two years; big deal,' was the reply Fairbanks gave, lifting his arms in the air with his palms open, as if to signify that it meant nothing. Then, pointing an accusing finger at Shelly, he sneered, 'And all the girls made fun of your friend because you said she farted - even bigger deal.'

Shelly now had tears in her eyes. 'It's worse than that. My friend …'

Again Fairbanks did not allow her to finish speaking. He yelled at her, 'Your friend couldn't take a joke. And you got your story straight to get shot of your husband and keep the house to yourself. And the two of you say you're having nightmares. You've never seen your friend lying there with half his brains blown out; you don't know what nightmares are.

'And while we were back at the nick getting our story straight, there's one copper saying, "But I was stood there right by you; he never said 'let him have it'." A right pain he was …'

This time it was Shelly that interrupted. 'But I thought you said he did say that.'

'I did not say that,' replied Fairbanks through gritted teeth.

Again Shelly asked, 'Well, did he?'

Fairbanks did not take too kindly to being quizzed in this way and he certainly was not going to take it from a little snip of a girl. 'That is not the point,' he barked back.

Shelly asked again, 'Did he say "let him have it"?'

Fairbanks now pushed his face as close to Shelly's as he could in order to be as oppressive as he could, and he bellowed, 'I told you, that's not the point. The point is …'

Shelly's reaction to somebody behaving towards her in an aggressive manner like this would normally be to cower away; but not now, not today: she interrupted and reacted in the same aggressive manner, and as she did so she raised her voice and asked again, 'Did he say "let him have it"?'

Shelly's sudden change of temperament took Fairbanks

by surprise. He now answered defensively, 'What he said and what he didn't say ain't the point. The point is …'

Again Shelly interjected; this time she screamed at the top of her voice. 'Did he say "let him have it"?'

'No, no he didn't say it,' Fairbanks screamed back and as he did so he burst into tears. As he then crumpled back into the chair, he put his head into his hands and he sobbed. Shelly slowly sat back down on her chair, and nobody said a word: the only sound that could be heard was the reverberation of Fairbanks weeping, and then after a few minutes through his tears he sobbed, 'You really don't get it, do you? If we told the story as it was, the worst he would have got would have been attempted theft.'

Despite the fact that Tilly despised Fairbanks and everything he stood for, she suddenly felt compassion for him as she asked, 'So what about your colleague? Surely his evidence was proof enough that the young lad did not say "let him have it".'

Fairbanks now spoke quietly, and through his tears answered, 'He didn't give evidence; we wouldn't allow it - and none of us ever spoke to him again. One of our own got killed and we wanted a result.'

At the police station the second police officer on the scene insisted that the young lad that Fairbanks had arrested had never said a word. 'He just stood there looking terrified. If he had said anything I would have heard him; I was standing right next to him all the time" were the words he said.

Due to his refusal to co-operate with his colleagues, he was cold-shouldered and it was suggested that he applied for a transfer. Police Constable Payne moved home and was transferred; he never in his entire career ever received promotion.

Tilly now spoke in a matter-of-fact way. 'But surely forensics would have shown that his accomplice shot your colleague. Would that not have been enough to secure a murder conviction?'

Fairbanks replied, shaking his head and with tears rolling down his face. 'You really don't get it, do you? First of all, the one with the gun was only sixteen; secondly, he had a Colt .455 Eley. The pathologist's report said he was shot with a bullet ranging from a .32 to a .38 - we were all issued with .32 Webleys.'

It fell silent as the realisation of what he was saying sank in. This was probably the most talked about trial in the history of British justice, and here and now the arresting officer with his tear-stained face was revealing details which nobody had previously ever dared to mention.

It was Shelly that broke the silence. 'So it was a policeman that shot your colleague.'

Fairbanks was now feeling like a rat trapped in a corner. He answered defensively, 'They were to blame, not us; not no one else. If they weren't on the roof, none of this would have happened; a copper was dead and they were responsible.'

Again Tilly was very matter-of-fact. 'But the bullet that killed him: forensic tests would show which gun it came from.'

Fairbanks was now staring at the floor as he stated, 'The bullet was never found. In the interview room the sixteen-year-old denied firing the fatal shot, but we managed to convince him to admit to doing so and killing my colleague and because of his age he would get clemency. They both got convicted of murder: the sixteen-year-old for killing my colleague and the eighteen-year-old for encouraging him to do it. Case closed; we got the result.'

Shelly had studied this case as a project she was doing at school and had always seen it as a miscarriage of justice, but had no idea of the extent of the fraudulent evidence by the police. The realisation that the police would withhold evidence and tell blatant lies in order to send an innocent lad not much older than herself to the gallows made her feel sick to the bottom of her stomach.

She now pointed an accusing finger at Fairbanks as she said, 'You stood up in court and swore the boys lives away! Are you proud of yourself?'

Grabbing her finger and pushing it aside, he replied sternly, 'You have no right to ask me that. Do you know what it's like to give evidence in court?'

Tilly was looking sorry for herself as she said, 'I know what it's like to give evidence in court. I told you, I did it once. I wasn't prepared to do it a second time.'

'Second time? What happened the second time?'

'They wanted to take my little girl away.'

'That's terrible,' Shelly said. 'I do not agree with what you did to your husband, but no one should try to take your daughter away. What happened?'

'My little girl got taken away from me, that's what happened,' answered Tilly.

'That's terrible. But why?'

Tilly found it difficult to choke back the tears as she answered, 'After the trial, Julie moved in with me. It was exactly what we both wanted; the two of us were living like a proper couple, not having to sneak around. We could now sleep together every night, and everything was ideal at first. Of course, the neighbours were gossiping, but why should I care? If they had lives of their own they wouldn't have time to talk about mine.'

'But why did they take your daughter away?'

'We started going out to bars regularly. Julie had a really bad drink problem. I never really noticed it when Stephan was with me, because we only met during the daytime when he was at work, apart from the evenings that we went out together when he would babysit.'

Fairbanks did not like what he was hearing; he looked down his nose at Tilly and sneered, 'You mean you left your husband at home with a baby while you went to the pub?'

'Men do have some uses,' Tilly replied sarcastically. Then she turned towards Shelly and began to explain; as if during her whole life she had carried this guilt, she needed to unburden herself and finally telling somebody who genuinely cared would rid her of this guilt.

'After she moved in with me, we had a number of babysitters. Julie always wanted to go to the pub; if we didn't go out she would go to the off-licence and bring home some wine. Most nights we would drink two or three bottles; then one night we got very drunk. I went upstairs to bed and left her on the sofa drinking. I was woken up by the smoke alarm. I could hear Hannah screaming. I ran into her room and picked her up, then ran down the stairs with her in my arms and out through the front door. When we got outside, Julie was already there, standing on the pavement. Hannah was coughing violently; then she started to vomit. By the time the fire engines arrived, the inside of the house was gutted, completely burnt out. It appeared that Julie had dropped a lit cigarette which had started the blaze; ironically, we had a tiff a couple of days previous about her smoking in the house when my little girl was around. Julie thought it was funny to call her over then blow smoke directly into her face. I asked her not to do it as it upset Hannah and was bad for her health. Julie just said, "Don't be stupid. I've been around smokers all my life and it's not done me any harm".

'An ambulance arrived and the three of us got taken to hospital. Amongst everything else I was given a blood test and informed that I was five times over the legal drink-drive limit. I was not even driving, so what was the point of that? And I got sick of hearing everybody say how lucky we were to have gotten out of the house unharmed. I knew that; why did everybody have to keep saying it?

'But my predicament did not end there. The house was not insured against fire. You don't ever imagine it will happen to you, do you? So not only did I have no home, but I had a huge clean-up bill coming my way. And believe me, that was only the start of my troubles. There was an endless queue of people wanting to give evidence that I was a bad mother.

'Social services wanted to take my daughter away. I couldn't face going to court and being on the receiving end of allegations, so I gave in; I haven't seen my daughter since.'

'What about your girlfriend Julie?' Shelly asked. 'She was a policewoman, and you said she specialised in domestic matters. Could she not have helped you?'

Tilly was now slowly shaking her head from side to side and with a deep look of sorrow in her eyes she answered, 'We moved into a bedsit. I kept crying all the time; Julie was going out drinking more than ever. I couldn't face other people, so I just stayed in the room. Then one day she just said, "This is not working out". Then she just took her belongings and went. I haven't seen her since. In the space of a few weeks I lost my husband, my lover, my house, and my daughter.'

Fairbanks seemed to take some kind of sadistic pleasure in her pain. He slowly and purposely remarked, 'Well, it serves you right; you neglected your daughter, you were a bad mother.'

'I didn't deserve to have my baby taken away.'

'Yes you did; you're nothing but scum and I hope you rot in hell.'

At that moment Tilly lost control. She leapt out of her chair and as she did so she slapped his face and screamed, 'I'll kill you, you bastard.'

Leaping out of her chair and pushing herself between them, Shelly yelled, 'Stop it! Please stop it; sit down, please sit down. He didn't mean it - you're not a bad mother.'

Tilly sat down. Her hands were trembling, she was perspiring and the tears were rolling down her cheeks, as she declared, 'He did mean it and he's right: I am a bad mother.

I loved my little girl more than anything in the world, and I put her second to everything else, and I am paying for it. Every single day I pay for my mistakes.'

Julie moved back into police accommodation; while she was living there she met Claire, a new recruit from the Midlands, and they began a relationship.

Hannah, without Tilly's knowledge, was adopted by a young married couple that lived just twenty miles away. She never attempted to make contact with either of them ever again.

A TRIP TO THE SEASIDE

Tilly had decided to go to the seaside for a couple of days, so she set off in her black three-door Peugeot 205, and headed for Great Yarmouth.

When she arrived at her destination, she booked into the largest hotel on the seafront, demanding a double room with a sea view.

As the bell-boy opened the door to room eighteen, she ordered him to bring to her room a bottle of house red and one glass straight away. She saw the young man as beneath her, and felt no need to be polite or treat him with any kind of respect.

Peter was the name of the bell-boy. He was working in the hotel temporarily and was trying to save enough money to go to university, not that Tilly cared; he was there to serve her and that was all she needed to know.

It took Peter just four minutes and forty-eight seconds to

rush down the stairs and return with a bottle of Portuguese red wine. When he arrived there the door was open, but he tapped on it lightly, as he was taught never to enter an occupied room until you are invited to do so by the guest. Tilly greeted him with, 'You took your time.'

Peter entered the room and removed the bottle and glass from the silver tray they were on and placed them on the bedside table. As he did so, he asked, 'Is there anything else you would like, Madam?"

Tilly replied abruptly, 'No, not right now. I will call when I want something. Close the door on your way out.'

She sat gazing through the window at the sea and drinking the wine at a rate faster than she normally would. Whilst sitting there, she began to reminisce about her time with Stephan, and remembered the reason she married him was because of his kind, considerate nature; she also found him appealing to the eye and he had won the approval of her friends.

If you were asked what appealed to you most about him, you would probably say his sense of humour that managed to see the funny side of most situations.

What Tilly liked most was his easy-going nature, which meant she had their relationship exactly the way she wanted it for the majority of the time.

They had only known each other for eleven weeks when

she moved into his cosy little penthouse flat with him. She had been back from America for four months now and did not like having to live back at home with her mother, so Stephan was her knight in shining armour.

For the first five years everything between them was bliss; he absolutely doted on her and their daughter, and it was plain to see they were his whole life.

But then she met Julie and, as their relationship grew, her marriage to Stephan suffered.

It was a warm summer evening and, whilst she was drinking a second bottle of wine, she decided to go for a walk. She left the room without bothering to close the door behind her.

As she was walking on the beach towards the sea, the urge to swim came over her.

The multi-coloured summer dress she was wearing had buttons up the front. Tilly undid them from the top to the bottom, then pulled the dress back over her shoulders and let it drop onto the sand. She then removed her undergarments and slowly strolled naked into the sea. When she got to the point where the water was above her waistline, she threw herself forward and began to swim as far away from the beach as she could.

MAY THE LORD HAVE MERCY

Tilly was now reduced to a quivering wreck, but even though Fairbanks took some kind of sadistic pleasure in seeing a person reduced to that kind of emotional state, he was not completely satisfied; he went in for the final kill, like a hunter homing in on his prey, but this time it was not physical, it was emotional. He pointed his finger at her and, with a look of total scorn, he stated, 'You got what you wanted; you wanted rid of your husband - he got put away, you got your result.' Then with a sneer he went for the jugular as he mocked, 'You must be feeling quite pleased with yourself.'

Shelly could sense the pain that Tilly was feeling. She looked at Fairbanks and said pleadingly, 'Please leave her alone. Can't you see she has suffered enough. We have all made dreadful mistakes; we all have our cross to bear.

Remember, you got an innocent boy convicted, but you don't seem bothered, and you call it a result.'

Fairbanks rose to his feet. Shelly feared his backlash, but when he gazed into her eyes she saw no anger, just sorrow. He turned his head and stared ahead of him. When he spoke there was no anger in his voice; he spoke softly and repentantly. 'You are right. I got my result, I got an innocent boy convicted. The doctor's report said that he had the mental age of an eleven-year-old. The case against him should not even have gone to court, but it did, and I got the highest commendation possible; but I wasn't the brave one. He always pleaded his innocence, and, at the same time, he, his parents and his sister kept their dignity. I will never forget the sight of the judge sitting there wearing the black cap. The words he uttered will haunt me forever: "You are nineteen years of age, and it is my duty to pass upon you the only sentence the law can pass for the crime of murder. You will be taken from this place to a lawful prison and thence to a place of execution, where you will suffer death by hanging and your body buried in the precincts of the prison in which you shall be last confined before execution, and may the lord have mercy upon your soul."

'All he did was climb onto a warehouse roof, and due to my evidence he received the death sentence. He must have been terrified as he walked into the grey cold stony execution room with his hands secured tightly behind his back. How must he have felt when he saw the hangman's noose, and the terror that would have run through his mind when he was escorted forward and the rope was slipped over his head and around his neck? How intense was the physical pain when the trap door was open and his body dropped? For how long was he hanging before he felt no more? Every time I close my eyes, every time there is a moment's silence, I hear his voice: "I ain't done nothing, I ain't done nothing" - then I hear the sound of the trap door opening and the crack of his neck. I have been trapped in this hell for so long.' The tears rolled down his face as he stared ahead of him, not looking at anything, just gazing into space.

Shelly was also gazing at nothing as she confessed with regret, 'I know how you feel. It was my fault. It was I that started the taunting of my friend. She did nothing wrong; in fact, she was the most pleasant person I have ever met, and despite that the girls at school made her life hell. I could have stopped it, but I didn't; I made it worse - I change a pleasant conversation we were having into an unbearable moment for her. How must she have been feeling as she ran from the dining room?

How alone and unwanted did she feel as a result of the constant torment she was made to endure?

'I remember when the police came to our school. They

looked solemn-faced. They had found her body and, as she was my friend and I was the last person seen speaking with her, they wanted to speak with me. A policewoman read out the note to me that she had left in her room; she did not sound angry, just very sad: "Dear Mum, I know what I am doing is wrong, and I am very sorry for all the hurt this may cause you; but I really can't take any more. I don't feel that I will ever be able to fit in. Please don't be sad. When I get to heaven I will give Daddy a big hug for you." Every time I close my eyes I see her face and the little red birthmark on the side of her neck; it looked just like …'

Tilly and Shelly now spoke together as they whispered, '… a little red star.'

Tilly now turned to face Shelly as the realisation sank in that the friend Shelly had spoken about was her daughter.

She sobbed. 'My Hannah, my Hannah, you killed my Hannah.'

The three of them now found themselves standing in a triangular shape. Each one of them was shivering with cold, whilst finding their bodies were soaked with sweat. The feeling of nausea they were now experiencing they found almost unbearable. Mist started to form around them; it slowly became thicker, so thick that they could no longer see each other. Then it suddenly cleared and a ghostly figure of a clown was standing amongst them. He wore bright shiny red shoes, and a multi-coloured striped jumpsuit. His face was scary, like the masks worn by the boys that killed Shelly's parents. The three of them wanted to get away, but they could not move: they were frozen to the spot, paralysed with fear. Then suddenly the clown placed his right hand underneath his chin and then, grabbing a piece of his skin, he slowly and deliberately pulled his face upwards until he had completely peeled it off, revealing the face of Shelly's friend Hannah. The silence was deafening; the sheer horror that was running through their minds and their bodies was unspeakable. Then Hannah spoke, but it was not Hannah's voice they heard, it was a tone they had never heard before. This was a sound of hatred and damnation. 'You told your tale extremely well. It is now time for you to tell it again.'

This is not the end